MW00453270

The Darkened Village

by John H. Watson

edited by Barry Clay

Other Novelettes, Novellas, Short Stories, and Books by Barry Clay

A Little Bit of Everything (an anthology collecting:)

The Case of the MelRoy Theatre
   Ghost
The Name of the Frame
With Whom I Had Been Speaking
The Dip Takes a Plunge
My Life of Crime
The Blood is the Life

Brushes with the Supernatural (an anthology collecting:)

The Scarecrow of Bachmeier Farm
She Is Not Dead, But Sleepeth
That Which Seethes Within
The Cost of an Exorcism
   The Road to Hell
   The Blood is the Life
   The Cuckoo
   The Antrix and the Aeoli

Misadventures in Childrearing

The Adventures of Romain Kalbris

Collisions

Speaking

The "Solid Ground" Series

The "Solid Ground" series includes two books, *Solid Ground* and *UnReformed*, and many smaller books and e-books exploring Christian beliefs from a layman's perspective for new believers and those who aren't Christian but are interested in understanding what regular Christians believe.

Solid Ground

Solid Ground includes all of the material below, all of which can be found in smaller books or e-books.

Why What We Believe Matters
The Bible
In the Beginning
Man
The Attributes of God
God's Plan
The Holy Spirit
Salvation
Angels and Demons
How It All Ends
Baptism
"Elementary Teachings"

God and Gold
Communion
To Sin or Not to Sin
Spiritual Authority
The Question of Slavery
Spiritual Gender Differences
Meet and Drink Issues
Why Bad Things Happen to
    Good People
Predestination and Free Will
The Theological Fight of the
    Centuries

UnReformed

UnReformed contains new material addressing Reformed theology, but also includes the following updated and expanded small books and chapters from *Solid Ground*:

The Theological Fight of the Centuries
Predestination and Free Will
Why Bad Things Happen to Good People
Salvation

The Darkened Village

Copyright 2019 by Barry Clay

With acknowledgment to
Sir Arthur Conan Doyle who created
such believable characters in
Sherlock Holmes and John H. Watson
that even today, some people believe they
really lived in Victorian England

And to James Nelson, who read the manuscript
and provided cogent critiques that
made the book a better one. Any remaining
failings are mine.

Table of Contents

EDITOR'S INTRODUCTION I

PROLOGUE 1

CHAPTER 1 7

CHAPTER 2 20

CHAPTER 3 27

CHAPTER 4 35

CHAPTER 5 45

CHAPTER 6 51

CHAPTER 7 63

CHAPTER 8 79

CHAPTER 9 86

CHAPTER 10 97

CHAPTER 11 105

CHAPTER 12 118

CHAPTER 13 127

CHAPTER 14 132

CHAPTER 15 143

CHAPTER 16 152

EPILOGUE 163

Editor's Introduction

When I presented to the public the novelette *The Case of the MelRoy Theatre Ghost* (which can be purchased as an e-book on Amazon.com or in the anthology *A Little Bit of Everything*, available in both softcover and e-book), I originally included an explanation of how I came in possession of what I eventually concluded was an unpublished manuscript of John H. Watson, M.D. Briefly, I described that I had bought a very old, elaborately crafted wooden box at an auction at a significantly reduced rate. I discovered, upon dropping it and splitting it wide open (like the klutz I am), that it had a false bottom in which the manuscript was nestled.

I was very careful in that explanation. I did not suggest that there were other manuscripts in that false bottom. Despite that caution, I received phone calls at my home (sometimes in the dead of night from eager collectors who have no understanding of time zones) hoping that I still had the box, or better still, more manuscripts. That alone was annoying, but when a clumsy attempt was made to burgle my home and the perpetrator was caught by a police patrol, I learned to my shock that the would-be thief was a private detective from London, England, who admitted under questioning that he had been hired to ransack my home by a wealthy collector in an attempt to find another manuscript by John H. Watson, MD. The fee he mentioned was breathtaking.

My wife and most of my children were frightened. (I say most of my children because my oldest son, then twelve years of age, thought this was terribly exciting and wanted to stay up nights in an attempt to catch another burglar.) I, of course, was alarmed. I deleted the explanation of how I found the manuscript and pretended that I was simply engaged in a Sherlock Holmes pastiche, a pastime in which many writers more able than I am have participated ever since Dr. Watson's copyright fell into the public domain and his distant heirs (he had no children despite having been twice married) had no further legal claim on royalties.

But now is the time to admit that there was indeed one more manuscript in that box: this one. I can confess this now knowing that my number is presently unlisted, we have moved, and this was the only other manuscript in the box.

You may wonder why it has taken so long for me to present this final manuscript to the public. There are many reasons.

First, the box must have been badly treated in its travels before its life ended on the cement floor of my garage. The box, while well made, was not waterproof. I suspect it was exposed to the elements more than once. Perhaps it was even dropped in a puddle or, worse, a bathtub. The ink on some of the papers had smeared to the point of being unreadable, and some sheets had become a lump of pulp. It took me no little time to assemble the money to pay a laboratory to decipher the writing and separate the pages. Laboratories do not come cheaply. Truth be told, it took me even longer to find a laboratory that would undertake such a task. Alas, even using the latest of scientific methods, including computer reconstruction, some pages remained only partially readable.

Second, this final manuscript was much longer and in worse shape than *The Case of the MelRoy Theatre Ghost*. Quite frankly, there were times when I was forced to insert my own prose into that of Dr. Watson's in an attempt to make the story readable. I did that with no little trepidation. I am all too aware that I am not of the same literary caliber as John H. Watson. I worry, too, that I may have inadvertently inserted inaccuracies or anachronisms into the story, but my only other option was to let this story remain unknown. That was something I was unwilling to do.

Third, I did not have the resources to confirm the validity of the manuscripts, and I hesitated to perpetrate a fraud on the unwitting public as I may have done in releasing *The Case of the MelRoy Theatre Ghost*. As I wrote (and then deleted) when I released *MelRoy*, I simply don't have the connections to ensure that the papers I found were bona fide manuscripts from the pen of Dr. Watson. The story seemed legitimate to me when I read it (meaning the parts that were legible), but I am only an amateur.

Added to all of this was the difficulty I had with my word processor, which diligently and insistently corrected Doctor Watson's British spelling into American. I nearly relented, but I then decided that I should not let myself by bullied by software that was intended to help me. Eventually, I convinced it to accept the British spellings. Any American spellings that remain were those I missed during my review of the manuscript.

Finally, I have this pesky, full-time job that pays the bills; family members who pretend to enjoy my company, and who certainly prefer to eat three square meals a day (along with the occasional late-night snack); friends I like to see from time to time; church events; and volunteer commitments to the local student orchestra I conduct; all of which consume much of my energy, so my free time was limited.

But diligent balancing of my commitments and hard work has now brought me to the point where I can present to the public (as Dr. Watson himself would have said) the following adventure.

I have read many of Mr. Holmes's later adventures as edited by others, only to be quite certain I have been reading a badly written and inferior imitation cobbled together by an author with more greed than ability, who hoped to capitalize on the fame of Sherlock Holmes and his chronicler. In these stories, Holmes and Watson are distorted caricatures of themselves and placed in situations so outlandish as to be laughable, if they weren't so painfully bizarre. In other words, they have been frauds.

I am all too aware that some may find me guilty of similar incompetence and immorality. I hope not. I have done my best. If I have failed, please, do not fault Dr. Watson. I am solely to blame for any inaccuracies you may find in his story.

And so, with some hesitation, but mostly with expectation, I submit the last manuscript from that irretrievably-damaged box in the hopes that it will be well received by the reading public and the fans of Mr. Sherlock Holmes and Dr. John H. Watson.

For I, certainly, am one of them.

Prologue

"I shouldn't let it stop me, Watson."

Startled, for I had been deep in thought, I looked up from the *Times* that I had been holding in my hands and said, "I beg your pardon, Holmes?"

Holmes was lounging on the settee in his dressing gown, his Meerschaum pipe in one hand, regarding me with a suppressed smile and a twinkle in his eye.

"I said, 'I shouldn't let it stop me, Watson."

"What on earth do you mean, Holmes?"

"Why, only that I would go ahead and commit the story to paper."

"Holmes, how could you possibly know what I was thinking?" Even as I said it, I remembered all too well how many times in the past my friend had performed similar feats of apparent legerdemain, reading my mind as if he were a stage magician, except that we weren't on a stage at all. Rather we were ensconced comfortably in the familiar surroundings of the sitting room in 221b Baker Street, where we both lodged that summer at the turn of the century after the untimely death of my second wife.

"Watson, old boy, it wasn't difficult. First, I could see that you had been reading the *Times*, or, I should more accurately say, I could see you *had* been reading the *Times* when the recent scandal so ably presented on its front page sent you into reverie. I surmised you were considering other scandals you have known. I was certain of it when you glanced at the rather ornate box I presented to you three birthdays ago, in which you now keep the notes of our past cases that you have not yet presented to the public. Your eyes remained there for nearly an entire minute, and I concluded you were recalling a specific case of equal, or perhaps greater, scandal. You then turned to look at the unusually large rodent skull adorning the bookcase, an admittedly macabre memento from the case which you once melodramatically christened 'The Giant Rat of Sumatra,' a case you further declared as one 'for which the world is not yet ready.' You looked back to the box, and you shook your head slightly, leading me to conclude that you had decided that the public is not ready for the scandal inherent in this case also, and, therefore, it was not ready for publication and the effort it would take to prepare it for your editors. At that point, I broke into your thoughts and said that I shouldn't let such considerations stop me."

I sighed and admittedly, ruefully, "Holmes, as always, you are entirely correct."

If he drew any satisfaction from my admission, it wasn't apparent. Instead, he waved the hand holding his pipe. "May I enquire what case you were considering?"

"Of course. It was the case prompted by the visit from the Reverend Jeremiah Clarke and his wife."

Holmes's face darkened. "Ah. I remember it well. I can understand why you hesitate to put it to paper. It was one of my most spectacular failures."

"Surely not, Holmes," I protested. "You handled everything from first to last brilliantly."

Holmes waived a hand. "No doubt, your reading public would agree with your assessment, but I chide myself for my scepticism and lack of foresight. Had I been quicker, I might have prevented a good deal of tragedy."

"No one could have foreseen what happened!"

"I disagree. I should have foreseen it," said Holmes, bitterly, and to my mind, unfairly. "I should have been quicker to see the obvious signs and slower to dismiss the first indications of foul play as inconsequential."

"Holmes, you are too hard on yourself."

His smile was slightly mocking. "I suspect Mr. and Mrs. Nithercott might rather say I am not hard enough."

"They did not fault you."

"They should have done."

I fell silent, and I could see my friend was brooding heavily, obviously remembering what befell the village of Wenlock Edge and the nearby Waltham Abbey and Arbury Hall. It decided me.

"Holmes, you have let the horrible events cloud your memory of your actions. You must remember that I was there. I will prove it to you. I will take your advice. I will assemble my notes and write the story. Upon reading it, you will see that you were in no wise to blame for what occurred."

The corner of his mouth turned up. "Watson, you are loyal to a fault, but I suspect such a feat is beyond even your literary powers if you insist on presenting the case factually and accurately. My memory is not so faulty as you state. I suspect we only differ in interpretation. While your accounts of our cases often have more drama and histrionics than I find palatable, if you write an unbiased and accurate account such as you have insisted on doing in the past, I fear your reading public may be forced to conclude—however unwillingly—that the nearly infallible Sherlock Holmes they have come to admire from your portrayals of me is indeed as prone to error as the next man." He paused for a moment, then added, "Though I will admit that the case has sufficient melodrama, not to say horror, that it should satisfy their apparently insatiable appetite for the bizarre."

I hesitated at his words, for a problem had occurred to me that, in my zeal, I had not fully considered.

"What is it, Watson? You seem suddenly unenthusiastic when, just a moment ago, you were brimming with confidence and aflame to write."

I was uncomfortable. "There are many good men and women like the Clarkes and the Nithercotts involved in this case. I am reluctant to name them and so many others who were victims of such frightening circumstances and for which they were not to blame. It was why I originally decided to leave my notes where they are."

Holmes waved a hand dismissively. "Change their names."

"But the locality itself will certainly indicate to those who live in the area who was involved."

Holmes interrupted. "Change the locality."

"I have never done so before."

"Perhaps you should do so now."

"But will the public accept such a distorted account?"

"I have no doubt that they will, if you explain to them in advance that you have done so and why. The account must be accurate, but you would no doubt agree, the names and localities are incidental to what occurred. Or write the case, but do not send it to your editors. Use it simply as an exercise to prove me wrong, unlikely though you may be to reach that goal. Or both change the names and do not send it to your editors. After all, your stated aim is to prove that I am not at fault, and surely you have earned sufficient funds from your previous accounts of our cases that any income you might gain from publication is only of mild interest to you."

This was certainly true. At this point in 1899, the fame of Sherlock Holmes and the royalties I had earned over the years from chronicling his adventures had left us both comfortably provided for, if not wealthy. Holmes had been consulted by rich and poor (the latter from whom he rarely exacted payment) and, of course, Scotland Yard would make use of his acumen when it could not bring a particularly difficult case to resolution. He was at a point where he could pick and choose the cases he would accept without fear of penury, and he was more likely to accept a case without regard to payment if it presented unusual features that would challenge his abilities. For my part, the fees from my practice and the remuneration from *The Strand* for my stories and novels had left me equally and amply provided with funds. The fact that we once again shared lodgings, and that I received income from my let on the house which I had formerly shared with my beloved Mary—with whom my time was far too short—and later with my cherished Violet, ensured that I had more money at my disposal than a man of frugal habits such as myself could comfortably spend.

"Holmes," I said slowly, "I will take your advice. I will review my notes and write the story, changing the names and locality. Then, I think, I will leave it with my literary agent after it is completed to be released, perhaps, at some undetermined date in the future when all the good people affected are dead and buried."

"I would suggest that seventy years, Watson, would be sufficient for all remembrance of the individuals involved to have faded from living memory."

"And if not, the change of names would provide additional protection."

"Agreed."

And this is what I did. I write this prologue looking at the manuscript of the novel I have christened *The Darkened Village*. The names previously mentioned are not the true names of the personages involved. If I, by chance, have accidentally used names of personages or places that exist, it is the purest coincidence. I assure the reader that the following is a factual account of what occurred, but all the names of people and places – and even some of the features of the topography – are pure invention of my own.

As I look at the manuscript, still uncertain what I will do with it, my heart is heavy. At my insistence, Holmes read the entire text, but his original assessment of his failure remains unchanged. He is convinced he could have been quicker to make his deductions and should have done more to prevent tragedy. It is this tragedy – near-tragedy, to be more accurate – that gave me pause before writing, and it gives me pause even now. I have never before written a prologue to any of my works. But I feel the need to explain to my public why I originally hesitated and why I eventually wrote, knowing I write a prologue to a story that my never be read by any living human being other than Sherlock Holmes, a man I call friend, and who averted more tragedy and horror than any other human being could have done.

I present in this manuscript *The Darkened Village*. May I never live to see a similar adventure.

Chapter 1

As I look over my notes, I see that it was during mid-September of 1886 in which began the events that I intend to relate. To the relief of all London, the brisk air of autumn had followed a warm and sultry August. The frequently dismal weather for which London is justly infamous had given way to a bracing and pleasant season that, as I made my rounds, added a spring to my step and buoyed my spirits. As I passed other pedestrians, I could see that they, too, were enjoying equally the change in climate that was so atypical of the capital of England.

Sherlock Holmes was still early in his career, and my association with him only five years old. My accounts of his early cases were published, but, while no longer completely unknown, he had not yet reached the height of recognition with the public that he was soon to have. I still lived with him in his spacious lodging at 221b Baker Street, which was under the care of his landlady, Mrs. Hudson, but my remaining time there was to be short. I had recently purchased a modest row home in which I planned to install a surgery and live in the upper stories with my intended, Mary Morstan, after our marriage. We had briefly considered marriage by clergy of the Church of England, but because neither Mary nor I had living relatives and neither of us were regular churchgoers, we decided that our union would be officiated by the local registry office without ceremony, with only Holmes and Mrs. Hudson in attendance as witnesses. When I expressed to my affianced that I was puzzled and surprised that she had selected a date in December for our wedding, she only smiled as if amused and said, "If we marry in December and so close to Christmas, you will have no excuse to forget our anniversary."

When I repeated her words to Holmes, he remarked, "Miss Morstan is a very practical, and extremely shrewd woman." And then he added with a twinkle in his eye, "Are you certain you want

7

to go through with your nuptials, Watson? She might prove to be too much for you." I believe his words were in jest.

It was early in the morning, and I had completed my Saturday rounds, attempting to relieve the suffering of the ill. I had been pleased to learn that the ointment I had found, composed of a natural but rare substance called wogonin, had in fact helped relieve old Mrs. Kelsey's occasional bouts of arthritis pain. It was gratifying to be so correct, and she was almost embarrassingly effusive in her praise of my abilities. I found myself hoping that modern science would discover other substances that would relieve the similar ills that plague mankind.

I was reading the paper about the recent transatlantic voyage of the RMS *Oceanic* and the previously unheard-of luxuries available to its guests. Holmes was smoking his pipe and handling his revolver in a desultory, abstracted manner. He had earlier bemoaned that there were no problems of interest, stopping just short of berating the criminal class of London for their lack of invention, and I could see the boredom in his partially closed eyes and enervative manner of his movements. I was about to suggest a brisk walk together in the streets of London, when the sound of Mrs. Hudson's footsteps could be heard on the stairs.

"Enter, Mrs. Hudson," called Holmes loudly enough to be assured of being heard through the closed door.

Our landlady entered and the good woman spoke, barely acknowledging the revolver in my roommate's hand. She had long practice with ignoring Holmes's eccentricities. "I beg your pardon, Mr. Holmes, Dr. Watson. There is a couple to see you. Shall I show them up?"

"By all means," said my friend. "My ennui is so deep that I believe I would welcome a commission to find a lost dog rather than remain idle another hour."

But Mrs. Hudson hesitated.

"Is there a difficulty, Mrs. Hudson?"

She seemed somewhat at a loss for words, and then decided herself. "No difficulty, Mr. Holmes. It's just that…."

"Yes?" Holmes prompted.

"Well, I thought you should be warned. The gentleman is a man of the cloth."

Holmes turned to me. "Well Watson, what do you think? Why might a man of the cloth have need of a consulting detective?"

"I am sure I have no idea," I replied.

"Indeed, neither have I. The day looks brighter – or at least more interesting." He turned to our landlady. "Show them up, Mrs. Hudson, and we shall soon know what brings them to our doorstep."

In a short time, the couple was ushered gently into our sitting room by Mrs. Hudson. "Rev. and Mrs. Clarke," our landlady announced and exited discreetly, closing the door behind her.

The vicar was young, handsome, and perhaps not yet thirty. His pale face was nearly round, with short brown hair that I suspected had been tamed into submission for this visit. His equally brown eyes promised a quick intellect that was perhaps equalled by a clear conscience, though he now appeared awkward and ill at ease. His skin had the smoothness of youth. Indeed, had someone told me he was not yet twenty, I would have credited it by his appearance alone, except that no youth could honestly wear a clerical collar at so young an age. He was dressed in black except for the sign of his office. He held a bowler hat in his hand as if he was afraid he might drop it.

Mrs. Clarke was stunningly pretty and modestly dressed in a deep lavender dress that was just short of touching the floor. The colour accented her pale skin. Her hat was made of the same, lustrous material. Her hair was nearly black and curled down both sides of her head becomingly. On the left side of her chest was a silver pin in a filigree design with a small stone the colour of amethyst in its centre. She glanced to her husband as if sensing his unease, and he smiled at her reassuringly.

"Mr. Clarke, Mrs. Clarke, please sit. Welcome to London." Holmes indicated the chairs opposite the settee. I took another chair as both our guests sat. "Or should I refer to you as Rev. Clarke, or perhaps Vicar?"

Rev. Clarke reddened as if he were a schoolboy. "Mr. Clarke is quite sufficient, Mr. Holmes. I have never been one to stand on ceremony or rank. And 'Mr. Clark' is, after all, quite proper as an address for a country vicar."

Holmes nodded, and I could see that he approved of this answer. "Very well then."

The vicar resumed his normal colouring and cleared his throat uncomfortably. "Thank you for seeing us like this, Mr. Holmes. We beg your pardon for intruding."

"Think nothing of it. You must have an extremely important reason to interrupt your planned holiday with a visit to me."

Rev. Clarke seemed startled. "I beg your pardon, Mr. Holmes. How did you know this was our holiday?"

Holmes pointed. "Your train tickets are poking ever so slightly from your pocket, and I can see from the date that they were purchased some time ago. Had you purchased them with the intent to see me, you would have wired in advance. Since it was a planned trip and Mrs. Clarke is with you, I assumed a holiday. Perhaps even an anniversary? Am I correct?"

The vicar was even more surprised. "You are indeed correct, Mr. Holmes. I met Mrs. Clarke here in London when I was still a seminary student. We return every year to the small tea shop in which we met and treat ourselves to their sandwiches and pastries."

Mrs. Clarke smiled, glanced at her husband, and spoke for the first time. "He quite stole my heart away at that first meeting."

Rev. Clarke smiled wryly. "An unlikely meeting between a poor student and the daughter of a peer, but a fruitful one."

The two seemed quite happy, and I found myself hoping that my Mary and I would soon match them. Holmes asked, "What has caused you to interrupt so felicitous an occasion to enquire of London's only consulting detective?"

Rev. Clarke's face darkened, and he once again looked uncomfortable. His wife reached over and squeezed his hand. Finally, he spoke, "I almost did not, Mr. Holmes. I was torn between my growing unease and the rational part of my mind which told me that my concerns were unwarranted, unreasonable perhaps. It was only this morning, when at my devotions, that I felt compelled to call on you."

Holmes's mouth twitched, and I could see he was enjoying one of the rare, unexpected pleasures in his life. "Watson, I believe this is the first time, and it will perhaps be the last, that I have been recommended by Divine Providence."

Again, Rev. Clarke's fair complexion reddened, but this time more from anger than embarrassment. His voice had a touch of censure in it when he said, "You mock me, Mr. Holmes."

Holmes shook his head. "I would never intentionally mock a man who has so recently come into such a large inheritance and spent so little of it on himself, but instead on others. I respectfully beg your pardon if I implied otherwise."

This time, both our visitors gaped at him. Rev. Clarke said, disbelief in his voice, "How could you possibly know that? The tickets I understand, but how could you know that I have recently come into money? Did you investigate me? How could you do so when you did not know of my coming?"

Holmes did not quite smile. "Mr. Clarke, no investigation was required except for the one I conducted in this room just now upon your entrance. Your suit is well mended and tended to with love, but it is noticeably shiny and almost threadbare in spots. Your wife, on the other hand, is dressed in the latest fashion. Her dress is so new I can hear it crinkle when she moves. The amethyst on her pin is quite real and shows no signs of wear that would indicate it to be a family heirloom. It is undoubtedly a new purchase. All this indicates new wealth and an inclination to spend it on others rather than yourself."

Mrs. Clarke entered the conversation a second time, this time with passion. "Oh, Mr. Holmes, you are absolutely correct. I have tried to tell him that he simply must dress better now that we can afford to do so, but he tells me there is so much poverty and suffering around us that it would be unchristian to do so. But me! He insisted on purchasing several new outfits for me. And this pin! If anything is unchristian it is the expense of this pin, but he insisted."

Rev. Clarke cleared his throat, "You are the daughter of a peer of the realm."

"No longer. Now I am the wife of the vicar of Wenlock Edge, and both happy and proud to be so." She looked at us. "His parishioners love him almost as much as I do," she informed us, and then returned her gaze to her husband, who was blushing even more fiercely than he had done previously. "I have never been happier."

I could tell that this connubial bliss, which I found so affecting, was beginning to wear on Holmes, whose opinion of the fair sex in general and marriage in particular was rarely complimentary. "But I presume to conclude that there is now a need for my services. May I know why?"

Rev. Clarke nodded. "Yes. Of course." He hesitated, then made an internal decision. "I can see from the observations you made here just now that laying our situation before you is the right decision. I had read some of your cases in *The Strand*, but I never would have dreamed to have need of your services; or having need, to be able to afford them; or being able to afford them, of making the request. But as I said, I felt compelled to lay my concerns before you."

He continued, "I hesitated because my concerns seem so banal and pedestrian that I was ashamed to voice them, but neither can I dispel the feeling of dread that lays heavily upon me, the suspicion of something quite wrong that presses upon my thinking, both in Wenlock Edge and the nearby abbey and at Arbury Hall."

Holmes spoke. "Pray, tell me, what weighs so heavily on your mind?"

He cleared his throat. "Mr. Holmes for the past month, perhaps more, several family pets and some small livestock have gone missing and...."

At this point, Holmes burst into laughter, surprising our guests and especially me, who knew him better and had rarely known him to surrender so completely to unrestrained mirth. We waited until his laughter subsided. "I must beg your pardon a second time," he apologized. with laughter still in his voice. He explained, "The irony was too rich. I had just commented to Watson that I was so bored that I would welcome a commission to find a lost dog, and here you are."

I feared Rev. Clarke would blush again, and indeed he did. "Mr. Holmes, I know how this sounds. A country vicar approaches you, not with concerns about a gang of thieves or an unsolved rural murder, but missing pets and animals. This is why I did not wish to come. Certain it was beneath you—a man of your growing reputation and even respected by Scotland Yard—to investigate such paltry occurrences, I vacillated in my decision to consult you. And yet, and yet, Mr. Holmes, something is wrong. I feel it when I walk the streets. I see it in the worried faces when I visit my parishioners. Even the owners of Arbury Hall, a wealthy, landed family that should have no concerns worthy of mention, even with them I sense a tension that is unspoken when they attend services. I see it in their manner. I hear it in their inflection."

He looked at us earnestly. "Perhaps you consider me alarmist, starting at shadows, credulous and gullible, but I have been three years in Wenlock Edge, and something is very, very wrong. You must believe me." He leaned back, having exhausted his fervor, and looked at Holmes to judge the effect of his words.

Holmes was silent, considering, when Mrs. Clarke, who had been regarding me intently said, "You believe us, Doctor Watson, don't you?"

Before I could answer, Holmes waved a hand. "I am afraid that Watson is overly susceptible to feminine charms and the promise of marital bliss."

She smiled at him. "But you are of a more sceptical nature, Mr. Holmes?"

"As suits my profession, Mrs. Clarke." His eyes twinkled at the riposte, softening his words.

Rev. Clarke re-entered the conversation. "Does this mean that you will not help us, Mr. Holmes? As you deduced earlier, I now have sufficient means to pay any fee you could possibly charge. Does this not interest you, Mr. Holmes?"

"Not in the least. I do not assume cases solely based on monetary considerations. And you do me an injustice. I have not yet refused your case. Before I commit myself one way or the other, I have questions that may help me determine if I can be of assistance."

"Ask them, Mr. Holmes."

"You say that family pets have gone missing."

"And other animals."

"How many in total?"

He seemed to consider. "Old Kirby Kent's terrier. The Nibleys' cat."

"She would jump to your lap and curl there, purring, if you visited," added Mrs. Clarke.

"The Morley ... dog. It was something of a mongrel. I could not tell you what breeds may have gone into its making." He thought some more. "The newborn kid from the Gresham farm."

"You're forgetting the piglet, dear."

"Yes. A piglet from the Bradshaw farm."

I could sense a sudden quickening in Holmes's interest. "Just one piglet?"

"Yes, Mr. Holmes."

"How many were in the litter?"

The question surprised our guest. "Oh, my! Eight or nine, perhaps. It was a normal litter."

"And the remaining piglets were still there?"

"Yes, and doing very well I understand."

"Odd." Holmes paused to consider. "Odd," he repeated. "I understand that sows will occasionally savage their young."

"I am surprised a city man like you would know that, Mr. Holmes. It has been known to happen, of course, but a sow that acts in that manner will generally attack her young indiscriminately."

"And, of course, there was no carcass."

"That is correct, Mr. Holmes."

He paused again. "Would I correctly assume that all these animals were small?"

Rev. Clarke appeared to have not considered the question previously, so there was surprise in his voice when he responded, "I believe you could say that Mr. Holmes. The kid was the biggest, perhaps, but it was very young and could have been carried by a child." He smiled, remembering something. "And indeed it was. The Greshams have four children, three of them girls, and not very large themselves, who treated it like a baby."

"Are these all the incidents?"

"As far as I know, but I could not swear there are not more."

"Could this not be the work of an animal? A dog gone wild, perhaps? Certainly, that would be the most reasonable explanation, would it not?"

"It was the first we thought of, Mr. Holmes – we meaning the townspeople. Once it was recognized that animals, whether pets or livestock, were missing on a regular basis, we assumed some kind of animal could be responsible, perhaps a Scottish wildcat or pine marten. Some even suggested a larger cat had escaped from a travelling circus. And, of course, we thought of wild dogs. But among our townspeople are hunters and trackers, and no sign of such an animal could be found by any of them. And there are no carcasses. There are only disappearances that we can attribute to no natural cause."

"Ah!" said Holmes. "And therein lies the rub, I gather, that has so darkened your village of Wenlock Edge?"

Rev. Clarke nodded. "Yes, Mr. Holmes. I am afraid my parish is a superstitious one. I might speak against such unfounded fallacies from the pulpit, but the congregants merely listen politely. Among themselves they will nod and attribute my lack of belief in the local superstitions to my youth, book learning, and inexperience."

"To what then do your parishioners attribute the cause of these disappearances?"

"The devil some say, though I explain the devil is far more interested in corrupting their souls than making away with dogs and cats. But most say it is the "mad monk" who, tradition says, walks the grounds of Waltham Abbey because he refused to leave when his priory disbanded. Supposedly, he begged and foraged for food, growing more and more desperate until he finally died there in the abbey from hunger. The story, of dubious origin, has become a legend that claims he has been haunting the grounds for centuries, still searching for something to relieve his insatiable cravings. No remains have been found, some say, because he eats the animals whole." He sighed. "There are other theories, each more fantastic than the last, though the mad monk appears to be the favourite of the gossips. I affirm, Mr. Holmes, that while they would all declare that they are good, Christian men and women, they believe these things with greater fervor and more certainty than they hold to the teachings of the Church of England."

"Yes," murmured Holmes, "that must be most distressing."

I raised an eyebrow at his tone, but, fortunately, our guests were too taken with their troubles to notice it. For Holmes, the teachings of the Church of England were not so far removed from tales of a mad monk wandering through an abandoned abbey.

After a pause, Rev. Clarke asked, "Well, Mr. Holmes? Will you help us?"

"If my poor skills will be of assistance, I will. I am not otherwise engaged, and your ... problem ... provides certain features of interest."

The thankfulness on his face and that of Mrs. Clarke were obvious. "You relieve our minds, Mr. Holmes."

My friend turned to me. "Watson, would you be free to provide your own inestimable assistance?"

"With pleasure, Holmes. Robbins has been asking when he can return the favour I provided when I substituted for him during his illness. I am confident that I can arrange with him to take my patients for a week."

"Then, yes, it is settled," said Holmes turning back to our guests. "With Watson at my side, I am confident that your problem is all but solved."

Mr. Clarke cleared his throat and again looked uncomfortable. "Do I pay you now, Mr. Holmes? I have my cheque book."

Holmes shook his head. "I will take payment only after I have solved your problem." And then he added modestly, "Assuming I solve it, of course. I would be loath to take remuneration for a problem left unresolved. Let us wait until we see the time and energy it will take to arrive at a satisfactory solution. As you say, this may be a very small problem. Indeed, I expect it will be."

"Then will you at least let us put you and Dr. Watson up in our home? It is small, but we have two spare rooms."

"Is there no inn?"

Mrs. Clarke said, "There is Mr. Holmes, and a good one for a village so small, but you would be most welcome to room and board with us and save the expense and inconvenience."

"Of that I have no doubt, Mrs. Clarke, but if we room and board with the parish vicar and his wife, we will learn only what the townspeople will say in your hearing, whereas if we room at the inn and have no association with you, paying for our food and drink as if we were mere travellers, people will speak more freely in our presence."

Mr. Clarke nodded. "I take your point, Mr. Holmes. There are many things that the parish vicar is the last to know." And then he looked at Mrs. Clarke and smiled ruefully. "Though his wife often receives more confidences when she visits." And he added, "The Nibleys' cat, for instance, has never curled into *my* lap."

It was the good lady's turn to blush, but she was silent.

"Then it is resolved," said Holmes. "You and Mrs. Clarke will resume your holiday without anxious thoughts, knowing that Watson and I will visit your town in the next day, or perhaps two as Watson must make arrangements. We will lodge in the inn as two gentlemen looking to escape the bustle of London and seeking the refreshment that only the country can provide. Or perhaps I will invent another reason. When we meet again, do us the favour of maintaining the pretence that it is for the first time."

"Should we pretend we do not know who you are? Your name is not entirely unknown, and it is most unique."

"By no means. It might help for your parishioners to know that Watson is a doctor and I am a detective. That in itself might loosen tongues. Gossip is often the detective's stock in trade, and I fear it is sometimes of more value than scientific investigation."

Our guests rose, and Holmes and I joined them. "One other thing, Mr. Clarke. You said that the disappearances were regular. What did you mean by that? Regular how?"

He seemed puzzled by the question. "Why, only that they did not happen every day, but often and close enough that they were remarked upon."

"When did these disappearances start?"

The vicar looked to his wife. She looked helplessly at her husband, then at Holmes. "Perhaps a month, Mr. Holmes? It is hard to say."

Her husband nodded.

"The people who have had pets or livestock vanish, are they related?"

Again, Rev. Clarke looked to his wife. She responded, "Mrs. Gresham is the younger sister of Mr. Nibley. Other than that, I know of no other relations between the affected families."

"Is there any ill will among these families? Or ill will concerning these families with others in your parish?"

They looked puzzled, and perhaps apprehensive. Rev. Clarke answered, "I take your meaning, Mr. Holmes, but, other than the occasional misunderstanding that occurs among a small populace in which everyone knows each other, I am unaware of anything that would provoke such hostility that it would result in actions against someone's pets or farm animals."

"Would you be aware of such, Mr. Clarke?"

"It is a small village, Mr. Holmes, and difficult to hide animosity of so extreme a nature I would think, even from the vicar and his wife." And then he added, "Though they would, of course, attempt to do so."

Holmes having exhausted his questions, our guests left arm in arm, leaving us alone. Holmes resumed his seat on the settee, and I in my chair.

"Well, Watson, what do you make of all this?"

"Surely, as you suggested earlier, it is an animal of some kind."

"That leaves no body?"

"It drags it away into the woods and consumes its kill there."

"That cannot be tracked or found by the village woodsmen?"

"They are, perhaps, not so competent as they believe."

Holmes nodded. "It is certainly possible. And yet, do you not think it is puzzling?"

"How so, Holmes?"

"If it is an animal, why does it not return more often? Surely, it must eat more often than five times in a month."

"There may be other disappearances that remain unreported, and perhaps it is dining off woodland creatures that no one would miss in between its forays into the village."

"Very good, Watson! That is certainly possible, and a logical thought. And the piglet? Why only one?"

"It was all it could take."

"And why did the sow make no noise?"

His question surprised me. "What do you mean, Holmes?"

"Picture the scene, Watson. A sow with a litter of eight or nine piglets. They remain close to their mother until they are old enough to be weaned. I am hardly a rural boy to know it from experience, but I cannot imagine a sow permitting any creature to make off with her young without some attempt to thwart the predator. Unless it was killed outright, the squeals of the piglet must have been horrendous, and certainly the mother would have fought for her young even if the piglet died without a sound. One would have thought that the piglet could not have been dragged away without notice, and yet that is apparently what was done."

I considered what Holmes said. "Could it be that there was such a fight, but we do not know it? The farmers may not have been at home when it occurred."

Holmes smiled. "Watson, you shame me. You are correct. There are many things we do not know, and as I have said in the past, it is dangerous to theorize absent of facts. We will visit Wenlock Edge together and obtain those facts. We will have one last case together before your marriage to the lovely Mary Morstan." His eye twinkled. "I hope she will forgive me for stealing you away from her."

Chapter 2

"But of course you must go," said Mary when I related the Clarkes' visit to her. "I quite agree with your clients. Something very odd is happening. I can think of no one better suited than Sherlock Holmes to plumb its depths, solve this mysterious occurrence just as he did for me, and bring you back to me quickly and unharmed."

Robbins was equally encouraging, if for different reasons. "I owe you a debt, old man. Had you not substituted for me when I was ill, I would have no remaining business. I'm delighted to oblige."

That evening, I returned to 221b Baker Street knowing I could inform my friend that I would be able to leave with him as early as the next day, if such a quick departure was agreeable to him. When I entered the building, Mrs. Hudson intercepted me. "Mr. Holmes asked me to warn you, he's with another client." She lowered her voice as if on the verge revealing a secret. "It's another curate, if you can believe that! It doesn't rain but it pours is what my poor, departed husband used to say."

"My goodness! Perhaps I should…"

But she interrupted me. "Mr. Holmes said that if you were to return before his client left, I was to show you up."

I hesitated, convinced it would certainly be awkward for me to appear, especially since Holmes would invariably decline another case when he had so recently engaged to leave London, but Mrs. Hudson, good woman, correctly understood my reluctance. "Mr. Holmes called me up himself not ten minutes after his new client arrived. He made it quite clear that you were wanted and shouldn't be concerned that you would be intruding. They're your rooms, too, after all, even if only for a few more months."

Well, that was certainly true. Mystified as to what all this might mean, I thanked our landlady and ascended the stairs. I knocked gently to announce my presence and entered our rooms.

20

Holmes, as was his custom, was on the settee. His guest was sitting on one of the wingback chairs before the fireplace, in which burned a comfortable fire. Both rose upon my entrance. "Watson, your return is most fortuitous. Permit me to introduce to you the Reverend Phineas Hambly, formerly of Wenlock Edge. Rev. Hambly, my associate, Dr. John Watson."

Rev. Hambly was an older man in his sixties, somewhat portly, but still with a full head of hair that was now grey and stiff with age. He was dressed in a deep blue, three-piece suit, the vest pocket from which dangled a gold watch chain. He wore no clerical collar, but he was dressed fashionably with a high collar secured by a gold bar. His eyes were bright and intelligent, and I could almost feel his quick appraisal of me culminating in his final approval. His grip was firm. With a medical man's eye, I felt certain that the reverend had many decades of good health in front of him before he would feel the infirmities of old age.

"Wenlock Edge?" I asked. "Surely not the same Wenlock Edge?"

"Yes, Watson, the same. Before your arrival, I explained to Rev. Hambly that Mr. Clarke and his wife were just here this morning and had already engaged me to look into a little matter." And then he added, "I'm afraid the good reverend was somewhat taken aback at me for not using Mr. Clarke's title of 'Rev.' until I informed him that Mr. Clarke himself approved my use of a less formal title."

Rev. Hambly spoke with the full, deep tones I have always associated with men of the cloth. "The younger generation, I fear, is far too informal." But there was a smile in his tone, and he added, "Perhaps it would be more fair to say that my generation was raised to be too formal."

"Not at all," I responded.

"I was not a little surprised to learn that my successor to the pulpit at Wenlock Edge had come himself, and I have been attempting to convince Mr. Holmes to pursue my enquiry as well as his."

Holmes added, "Rev. Hambly explained that he retired from ministry three years ago and was succeeded by Jeremiah Clarke."

"A bright lad," affirmed the reverend in his solid voice. "Perhaps a shade gullible, but nothing that experience won't cure. He has a true pastor's heart for his flock. I expect him to go far in the church."

Holmes continued. "I have not informed Rev. Hambly on what matter we have been engaged." When he said this, I noticed an edge to Holmes's tone that I suspected went unremarked by our visitor. I rather thought that Holmes might be warning me to say nothing of our clients' reason for their visit. Such a warning was unnecessary, and I wondered at it. Holmes surely knew I would no more reveal a client's reason for calling on him than break a medical confidence.

"Quite right of you, Mr. Holmes. You must protect your client's privacy. I will ask Jeremiah when I stop at Wenlock Edge on my way home if there is anything with which I can help."

"Oh," I said. "You don't live at Wenlock Edge then?"

He shook his head firmly. "Certainly not. I can think of no more annoying business than a man to have his predecessor in the same village, attending his sermons, and perhaps being used in unfair comparison by those in the congregation who are given to criticism, for there are always some given to easy grievance, even in the church. When I retired, I did so far enough away that I could attend services elsewhere, but close enough that, should Jeremiah want advice or need me to assume the pulpit when he took a sabbatical, I would be available."

I could not but think what a thoughtful arrangement that was.

Holmes said, "You might remember Mr. and Mrs. Clarke mentioning Arbury Hall in passing, Watson."

"I do."

"It is concern for the residents of the Hall that has prompted Rev. Hambly's visit."

"As I was telling Mr. Holmes, the Arburys have been staunch members of the church for many years, but I have been

22

informed that, of late, Lord Arbury has absented himself from services."

"And this was as far as we had gotten before your timely appearance. I was on the verge of expressing my surprise. A decline in church attendance is hardly a reason to hire a consulting detective." Holmes almost smiled. "Perhaps he simply does not care for Mr. Clarke's sermons."

"I hardly think that is the case. Those sermons I have had the pleasure of hearing from Jeremiah during his apprenticeship in Kent were excellent, almost riveting. Certainly, they were better than mine." He paused a moment before continuing. "I was uneasy with Lord Arbury's sudden change of habit. I am told Lady Arbury and the family still attend, but without Kenton – Lord Arbury that is. I suspected a rift of some kind among the family. Naturally, I called on Lord and Lady Arbury to enquire of their welfare. Retirement does not prevent a man from continuing to care for those he knows, and my relationships with Lord and Lady Arbury were supremely cordial. I was often at the Hall at their invitation, and I spent many pleasant hours discussing philosophy, politics, and even religion with Lord Arbury."

He shifted uneasily. "Kenton refused to see me. At first, I thought I had misheard. But, no. Travers, the butler, was most apologetic. Adelia – that is Lady Arbury – she was more welcoming and agreed to see me. But it was not soon after joining her in their sitting room that I grew even more concerned. She was proper and composed, but to my eye, she seemed strained and pressed. After some prompting, she finally told me that her husband has taken to making trips to London, sometimes for several days, offering no explanation for his visits before his departure or upon his return. When I offered my assistance, Lady Arbury thanked me for my concern, but she told me she suspected the reason. Indeed, it was obvious."

"And that reason?"

Rev. Hambly sighed. "The age-old story: she suspects another woman."

"A not unreasonable hypothesis. Given that Lady Arbury is likely correct, for what reason would you wish to engage me, Rev. Hambly? How can I possibly help in such a painful, but mundane situation?"

"I would like to hire you to find that woman, Mr. Holmes."

I'm not sure which of us was more surprised, me or Holmes. "To what end?" my friend asked.

"I wish to speak with this woman. She must be persuaded to release her hold on Kenton. While his children are grown, and his oldest married, he is still a father. In the eyes of the church, he is married. He made vows before God to cling to his wife, for better or for worse. I am witness to the fact that the Arbury's had a happy marriage, where love was reciprocated and mutual respect obvious. I want to return them to that connubial bliss in which they have lived for so many years."

Holmes tapped his fingers together in front of his chin before replying. "A laudable motive," he finally said, "but I suspect such an appeal will be fruitless. Certainly, this woman, if she exists, cannot be unaware of Her Ladyship's existence."

Our guest sighed again. "I suppose you are right, Mr. Holmes, but I am conscience-bound to make the attempt."

For a moment, there was no sound in the room but the quiet crackling of the fire.

"Will you take the commission, Mr. Holmes?"

Holmes shook his head. "As I explained earlier, I am already committed to the small problem presented to me by Mr. and Mrs. Clarke. I intend to depart for Wenlock Edge as soon as Watson can arrange to accompany me."

"But Mr. Holmes, the sanctity and happiness of a home lays in the balance."

"No doubt." Holmes cocked his head and examined Rev. Hambly. "May I suggest one or two reliable detective agencies who can, without doubt, find this woman – or uncover whatever reason His Lordship has for visiting London. We cannot be certain a woman is involved, after all."

It was the reverend's turn to shake his head. "I understand. He rose from his chair, perhaps a little disappointed. "I can find another agency on my own." After a pause, he added, "Is there no hope? Is there anything I can say that will make you reconsider your answer, Mr. Holmes?"

"I am afraid that my answer is final, Rev. Hambly, though I can do this much for you: if in the course of my investigation for the Clarkes I find some indication that will help you, I will provide it to you. I have your address on your card."

"Then that is all I can ask. Thank you, Mr. Holmes. You are a man of honour, and I understand your decision." He nodded to me. "Dr. Watson."

And we saw him to the door.

When we returned to our seats before the fire, Holmes asked me for the second time that day, "Well, Watson, what do you make of this visit from still another client?"

I considered. "He seems a courteous old gentleman, concerned for the marriage of those he considers friends and former members of his congregation. He seems well provided for in his retirement, and not the least bit jealous of his successor. I am surprised we heard no mention of a Mrs. Hambly during his visit."

"Ah, Watson, ever the romantic!"

"But, may I venture, this is not the kind of case that I would think would interest you."

He nodded, smiling slightly. "You know me well, Watson. No, the case does not interest me in the slightest. It has no aura of mystery, nor does it provide some unusual feature to challenge the intellect. Even if I were not already engaged on another problem, I would have declined it."

"I find myself surprised that you kept Rev. Hambly until I returned."

"Ah! That was for an entirely different reason."

"What was that, Holmes?"

"Does it not strike you as odd that within twelve hours, we've had two visitors from Wenlock Edge?"

"It is a strange coincidence."

"Coincidence? Is that all you think it is? I am not as well-known as all that, though if you continue publishing your rather dramatic and fanciful accounts of my cases, perhaps someday I will be."

"What else could it be?"

"What else indeed? That is the question. For this reason, I kept the reverend here, long after I would normally have entertained him, hoping to elicit some indication to its answer."

"Perhaps like Jeremiah Clarke, he has read my accounts in *The Strand*."

"He did not say so, but that possibility cannot be discounted." A faraway, detached look appeared on Holmes's face. "Perhaps there is more to the mysterious disappearances of animals in Wenlock Edge than meets the eye." And then, as if shaking of the fancy, he rose and said, "Come, Watson, perhaps this is, as you say, nothing more than coincidence. Perhaps it is simply another indication of Divine Providence at work! Let us leave speculation behind. Will you be able to leave with me on the morrow?"

"All has been arranged."

"Then, we have packing to do."

Chapter 3

With Robbins more than willing to stand in my stead for a week—and more if necessary he assured me—and with Mary promising me that she was well able to bear up under my absence in what was obviously a good cause, I accompanied Holmes on the first Pullman scheduled to stop at Wenlock Edge. We had both packed lightly and carried our luggage with us, and though I doubted I would need it, I brought my physician's satchel filled with the most commonly used of my medicines and implements. Holmes said no more about the case on our journey, instead informing me of his intention to write a monograph on the methods of deducing from ash the type of cigar that a man had been smoking. His earlier monograph, using the stride and the depth of footprints in different soils to determine the height and weight of the person leaving them, had been well received, if not as widely read as he had hoped.

The station that serviced Wenlock Edge was a spartan building, hardly more than a cottage, made partially of weather-beaten brick and roughly hewn lumber and attended to by a wizened man significantly past his prime who regarded us with interested, grey eyes. He identified himself as Enoch Difford, station master.

"Wenlock Edge?" he repeated at our enquiry. "We have few strangers looking for Wenlock Edge these days. Used to be that the Arburys had visitors every weekend when they were in residence, but now they keeps to themselves."

"The Arburys?" asked Holmes.

"Aye. The Arburys still own much of the land hereabouts that t'aint in the village. Many's as still works in the great Hall and in the lands, though not so many as once was. Come down in the world a bit, they have. Mr. Arbury keeps to hisself. Leaves his wife to do the work."

And he continued, "Now, there's still some *goes* to London from time to time. The vicar and his wife was just there."

"Indeed," said Holmes as if he didn't know that himself, "we must call upon them during our visit."

Mr. Difford squinted at us, suspicion twisting his face comically. "An' why did ye say ye was here?"

Holmes was prepared for the question. "We didn't, but I am preparing to write a monograph on the disparate types of soils in England and how to recognize them. I am looking forward to the quiet of the English countryside, as well as samples of its soils, to inspire me. Watson here is taking a well-earned vacation from his practice prior to his scheduled marriage, and he will provide company and distraction. We are looking for a rest."

"Aye," he said, though he didn't appear completely satisfied with the explanation. "Rest is what ye should have here. Not much else about." He nodded. "Young Symes there will see to ye."

Joseph Symes proved to be all of seventeen years and, to judge from the length of his patched pants that did not quite hide his ankles from view, growing faster than he could be comfortably clothed. He had red hair, a freckled face, and a ready smile. His carriage, if the open cart could be dignified with that name, was pulled by two brown horses that seemed to my unpractised eye to be better fed than their owner. During the hour-long trip, with Holmes on one side of the seat beside the driver and I on the other, we learned that he was the oldest of ten children. He met the train whenever he could in the hopes of earning extra income, most of which he gave to his parents. He was disarmingly cheerful for a young man whose life seemed a hard one to a man such as I who had lived in the comforts of London for the last five years.

At our request, he recommended The Good Lady inn, grinned and added, "It be the best 'cause there t'aint another one."

In comparison to London, Wenlock Edge was painfully small, though I was to learn later as I travelled more, it was not so small as some of the primarily rural villages that dot England. Its homes seemed oddly bent as if from age and more often than not were built from irregular stone instead of the brick so prevalent in London. Its streets were narrow and, at times, twisted as if uncertain in which direction they intended to head. The glass in the windows was clear but uneven, distorting the view of the interior like a carnival mirror. The roofs were unvaryingly shingled with slate. We passed many members of the populace in the streets as we rode to our lodgings. Their clothes were faded and often grey in colour. The sight made me to be thankful that I could afford a wife and – I hoped eventually children – in a profession that alleviated human suffering and demanded no small modicum of respect.

And it made me appreciate that I could make a home in the modern metropolis of London, capital of the greatest country in the world.

Wenlock Edge was nestled in a valley and surrounded by fields and woods. Above the town could be seen two large structures on either side of the hills, both partially hidden by trees. From the look of decay and disrepair that was visible even at a distance, I took the first to be the abandoned abbey, Waltham Abbey. The other I concluded to be Arbury Hall, home of the Arburys. To my eyes, it seemed windswept and lonely, barely more alive than the forsaken abbey. Both structures brooded over the village as if disinterested in its welfare and concerned only with their own demise, one in the distant past, and the other anticipated in the near future.

Our driver deposited us in front of The Good Lady and thanked Holmes profusely for the generous tip he added to the payment he requested for the ride. "If ye need to go somewheres else whilst here, ye're to ask for Joe, and I'll be pleased to be at yer service."

We entered the inn, which proved to be a larger establishment than one would have guessed from its front. There was a bar, before which were stools and behind which was a woman of perhaps forty-five, in the process of cleaning glasses with a rag. She was plump, her greying hair tied in a bun. There were no fewer than twenty rectangular tables with rough chairs around the room, which had a fireplace at one end. At this time of day, the inn was empty save for this portly woman behind the counter. When she saw us, she called, "Ivor, we have guests!" She used a voice that she could reasonably expect to be heard throughout her establishment.

She set down her work, dried her hands in a towel, and introduced herself. "Agnes Nithercott, at your service gentlemen. Will ye be needing two rooms?"

"Yes," said Holmes.

"An' for how long if I may ask?"

"You may ask us, but we are uncertain of the length of our stay, though we anticipate a week, perhaps. Hopefully, we can room and board here. Do I have the pleasure of addressing the 'good lady' herself?"

She blushed with pleasure. "Aye, that ye do." She lowered her voice conspiratorially. "We thought to name it after me husband, but then we thought 'The Grouchy Man' wouldna get as much business."

At that, her husband entered from a door to the side of the bar. He was a broad man, and despite what we had been told by his wife, of welcoming countenance. On seeing us, he showed every indication of surprise. He said to his wife, "I thought ye be jesting." He said it with a little wonder in his voice, as if he wasn't certain we were real.

"'Tis God's own truth. Two guests, and each wantin' a room."

"Aye, I see it be that. Welcome to our inn. I be Ivor Nithercott." He held out his hand, and both of us took it in turn. "And ye've met me wife."

"That we have. My name is Sherlock Holmes. My companion is Dr. Watson."

"I beg pardon for me surprise. We get few visitors, and none this time of year since afore me da' died. What brings ye to Wenlock Edge?"

Holmes repeated what he had told the stationmaster. "So, ye be a writer?" asked our host, attempting to conceal the fact that he considered writing a monograph on soil to be somewhat daft.

"Well, I write upon occasion. Truth be told, it is Dr. Watson who is the writer. I am a consulting detective."

Both of our hosts looked puzzled, and Mrs. Nithercott asked, "What be a 'consulting detective?'"

"A man who investigates the facts and the clues surrounding a crime or a mysterious circumstance, and uncovers the truth until there is no mystery remaining."

She glanced at her husband, then turned back to us. "I never be hearing of such a thing. Do such things really exist?"

Holmes smiled. "They do, indeed."

I added, "Mr. Holmes has been consulted by no less an entity than Scotland Yard. I have had the honour of providing assistance to him for one or two of his cases."

"It is Watson who has written of some of them, rather luridly, and his reminiscences have appeared in *The Strand*."

I could tell that both Mr. and Mrs. Nithercott were impressed to have such people in their inn. For my part, I was embarrassed to be so forthcoming. I rather felt as if we were boasting, but it was part of Holmes's plan that we quickly establish his vocation as a detective in the hopes of obtaining information more readily and more willingly from the townspeople. This expectation was validated when it had almost immediate success with our hosts.

After another look to her husband, and a nearly imperceptible nod from him, she said, "Perhaps, Mr. Holmes, ye can help us."

"It would give me great pleasure to be of service, Mrs. Nithercott. How may I be of assistance?"

She hesitated in an unconscious imitation of Jeremiah Clarke, then decided herself. "Well, I'm sure it be not such an important thing to someone from London, but we've had some disappearances here in Wenlock Edge."

Homes, who I knew to be an accomplished actor, raised his eyebrows. "My goodness. Who has disappeared?"

The good woman seemed mortified to answer, and it was her husband who spoke. "Not 'who', Mr. Holmes, but 'what.' It be an odd thing, but we be having animals disappear."

And from them we learned the same information we had learned from Jeremiah Clarke and his wife. But during the narration given to us by the Nithercotts, we were also exposed for the first time to the anxiety to which the Clarkes alluded during their visit at 221b Baker Street.

"There's none that believes Alexander has run off. Why, since the death of Mrs. Kent, he's followed Mr. Kent everywhere. I keep a bone for him for when his master stops in for a pint or a meal."

"What do you believe happened?"

Mr. Nithercott responded, "If it were only one animal, we'd have thought a pine marten or weasel. But there be so many."

Mrs. Nithercott nodded. "There be somat evil here, Mr. Holmes, mark my words."

"Hush, Mother," said Mr. Nithercott, for at that moment a young girl of perhaps five years of age entered from the same door from which Mr. Nithercott had appeared. Mrs. Nithercott immediately assumed a more cheerful expression. "Lily, come meet our guests." Both looked at her with no little love mixed with pride.

The child beamed at us. "We almost never get guests," she said. She still had the plumpness of childhood. Here hair was thick and black, and her eyes were large and matched the colour of her hair.

Mr. Nithercott said, "Lily, this be Mr. Sherlock Holmes and his friend, Dr. Watson."

"How do ye do," she said, seriously. She looked at me. "Are ye a real doctor?"

"I am," I assured her.

"Me dolly be feeling poorly," she informed me solemnly.

Her mother, embarrassed, almost spoke, but I forestalled her by crouching on my haunches so her daughter did not need to look up at me. "Then I should be delighted to examine her in the hopes of providing something that will help her to feel better."

"Mr. Holmes be a detective," interrupted her mother. This seemed to be a new word for her daughter, and seeing the puzzlement in her eyes, she added, "He be going to help us find out where all the animals be gone."

"Oh, goody!" she exclaimed. "Will ye find Blackie?"

Her mother explained to us, "Blackie be the Nibleys' cat I told ye of."

Holmes, following my lead – but to my mind reluctantly – bent down. His movement was unexpectedly stiff and devoid of the grace that normally accompanied his actions, and I was reminded that his experience with children was limited to Wiggins and the so-called Baker Street Irregulars, all of them older than this girl and all of them boys. He cleared his throat. "I will do my best."

If the girl was aware of Holmes's suddenly wooden manner, she gave no sign. "Blackie be the bestest cat I know."

"Then I will do the best I can to find him."

Her face twisted and she said, disgust plainly in her voice, "Blackie be a *girl*."

With as much surprise as humour, Holmes's mouth twitched, and I was convinced that this little girl had made a complete conquest of my friend by her innocent disdain. "Then I shall do my best to find *her*."

"Let me show ye to yer rooms," interrupted Mrs. Nithercott a second time. Mr. Nithercott took his daughter's hand, and they both disappeared back through the door from which they had entered.

A narrow, steep stairway on the side of the house opposite the fireplace provided access to the first story. Our rooms, while somewhat smaller than those to which we had become accustomed at 221b Baker Street, were clean and adequate for our needs. Both had one window and contained rope mattresses suspended from unornamented wooden bedsteads. Both rooms had a small chest of drawers for clothing and a stand with a pitcher and bowl, over which hung a mirror. A rough chair stood in one corner of each room. Mrs. Nithercott assured us that she would bring water as soon as we were situated in our lodgings. Dinner, she informed us, could be served at any hour after five and before ten, the times when the locals were expected to frequent the inn.

After unpacking my belongings, I joined Holmes in his room.

"Are you well arranged, Watson?"

"Yes, Holmes."

"Our lodgings are perhaps a little spartan, but they will suffice."

"I have had worse during the war."

"I'm certain of that, old man. What do you make of our hosts?"

"They are the salt of the earth, and their daughter is charming."

"Yes, it's not often I am so thoroughly chastened by someone who does not stand as high as my waist."

"Holmes, I suspect that she is their only child, and at their ages, probably unexpected."

"My experience with children is limited, as much by choice as from any other cause, but I deduced that myself." And then he added, "But I have learned one thing of importance. If I do not find Blackie, I shall fall precipitously in her estimation. She is already somewhat disposed to discount my abilities due to my ignorance of the cat's gender. Come, we must ready ourselves to join the townspeople who come for dinner to see what we might learn, and do everything we can to forestall the catastrophe of disappointing her."

Chapter 4

Being too early for dinner, we enquired as to the location of the vicarage, explaining that the stationmaster had recommended the vicar to us as someone who traveled to London from time to time. Receiving directions from our hostess, we walked the streets as she indicated, Holmes in his deerstalker and inverness and I with my stick.

In a short time, we left the more crowded portions of Wenlock Edge behind. The houses here, some of them nearly hovels, were surrounded by poorly tended lawns and gardens, their extremities occasionally bounded by wooden fences, some of which still showed signs of having been whitewashed. An infrequent home would show signs of more persistent upkeep, but the overall impression was one of poverty. The contrast to London and Baker Street was stark. Many of the gardens sported more weeds than flowers. I could see extensive vegetable gardens spread out behind most homes, and these were better tended, no doubt from necessity. I pictured the ladies of these homes canning in jars the produce that could not be immediately eaten, as my mother had done in my childhood.

The vicarage, however, was in better repair. Standing sturdily in the plot beside a church of brown stone that was by far the largest and most impressive building we had seen so far in Wenlock Edge, the vicarage was made of the same stone and presented to those who approached a wholesome, fresh appearance. While not as tall as the nearby church, which had a small graveyard surrounded by a fence of iron, the vicarage had two stories, three dormers jutting from its roof. Its yard was green and lush. Its garden, even so late in September, still showed some vibrant roses and crimson Cana Lilies that, I suspected, would not last many weeks longer. The fence was wood and freshly painted white. A walk made of the same brown stone as the church led to the front door, which was painted red, and on which Holmes knocked. Mrs. Clarke opened the door.

"Mr. Holmes and Dr. Watson, how good to see you again. Please, come in." She had forgotten that she was to pretend not to have met us previously, but as there were no witnesses, I determined that there was no harm done. We entered, and Mrs. Clarke shut the door behind us. "Jeremiah is in his study, working on this week's sermon. I'll fetch him."

I said, "You have a charming vicarage, Mrs. Clarke. It must consume much of your time to maintain it."

"It is much larger than we require, as we have yet to have children. But you are incorrect to say that it consumes my time. My husband has been hiring the local men and women, particularly those who are the most in need, to provide them opportunity, for to give them money for no reason would be to insult them unforgivably." She smiled at a thought. "It is beginning to task my ingenuity to no small extent, and that of my husband, to find work that needs done."

"Perhaps the church could require some attention," suggested Holmes.

"Indeed, that is our thinking, but church repairs must come from church funds, and not our own, lest we be accused of putting on airs or, worse, providing charity." She sighed, but not heavily. "Please, let me inform my husband that you are here."

Mrs. Clarke showed us into the sitting room, a comfortable room whose furniture must have served many generations of vicars. Several bookcases lined its walls, and Holmes studied them while we awaited our host. "An eclectic lot, Watson," he informed me. "Theological treatises, of course, from Calvin to Augustine to Arminius. I see the expected histories by Gibbons, Herodotus, and Josephus that are worn as if read repeatedly., but I also find, Tennyson, Browning, and Dickens. Mr. Clarke is a well-read curate." I knew that Holmes never read poetry or fiction, and I was somewhat surprised he even knew the names of these justly famous authors. He had declared to me on more than one occasion that the human mind could only retain so much, and it was irresponsible to clutter it with twaddle such as fiction, no matter how well written or socially important. He, at least, had no intention of stocking his mind with anything that would not provide him with information that would help him to better perform his chosen vocation.

Our host joined us with his wife. Unlike his wife, he remembered that he was not to have met us previously. "Good afternoon," he said jovially. "I am Rev. Jeremiah Clarke, and you've already met my wife Margaret. It's rare we get visitors in Wenlock Edge. How can I help you?"

But once we determined that there was no one in the house but ourselves, we abandoned the pretence of having just met.

"We have met the Nithercotts and their daughter."

"Lily is a dear," said Mrs. Clarke.

"And exceptionally bright," added her husband.

"Watson thought she was unexpected."

The vicar nodded. "Mrs. Nithercott had thought herself barren, like the biblical Sarah, and then Lily came along."

"She is the apple of their eye," his wife added.

"So I observed," said Holmes. "However, I am here to report progress. Mr. and Mrs. Nithercott have already mentioned the disappearances of animals to Watson and me. They have asked for my assistance, and I have agreed to provide it. There is no subterfuge needed to account for our investigation into the disappearances. Should anyone ask, you can say that I called on you, hoping you could provide additional information, for that is indeed why I am here." And then, as an afterthought, he said, "It may surprise you to know that we had a visitor yesterday evening from Wenlock Edge the same day that you called on us."

Both of them smiled. "Phineas – that is Rev. Hambly – stopped by on his way from London to apprise us of that fact. He spoke very highly of you." Rev. Clarke added mischievously, "Apparently, you surprised him by wishing him well on his new regimen."

Mrs. Clarke said, "He was as impressed as we were that you could know so much about a man simply by looking at him."

Holmes waved a hand. "A simple deduction, made from the changes in the notching of his belt, the most recent of which had not yet formed a crease, not to mention the loose fit of his collar. Both indicated that he had lost weight, and that recently. He appeared to be in robust health for a man of his age, and I discarded illness as a possible explanation, leaving me with the near certainty that Rev. Hambly was dieting and achieving a modicum of success."

"Phineas has been fighting that battle as long as we have known him," Mrs. Clarke informed us.

"Given that he asked, did you explain why you engaged me?"

"Of course." And then a look of worry crossed his face. "Did I do something wrong, Mr. Holmes?"

"Not in the slightest."

Rev. Clarke was relieved. "I could see no reason not to reveal the causes of my concern, and I only hesitated to do so for the same reason I was reluctant to call on you. It all seems so... inconsequential. When we explained the reason for our call, he was doubtful that it was anything more than a wild animal, but he was too well bred to suggest that we should not have bothered you with such a trivial problem. Rather, he asked us to tell you that if you needed any help from him, you should not hesitate to ask for it. We suggested that he stop by The Good Lady himself. He was vicar of Wenlock Edge for nearly twenty years, and he may have knowledge of its history that can help."

"We will look forward to his visit and any information he can provide."

"And we, of course, are ready to be of any assistance that we can."

"As to that, there is indeed information that can help speed our enquiry. Can you provide directions to all the homes where animals have disappeared?"

"Certainly," said the vicar, and he and his wife sketched a rough map of the village and handed it to Holmes, who looked at it intently.

"These homes and farms are too dispersed in location for us to visit them all today before the sun sets, but I see that the Nibleys have a home not far from here and close to The Good Lady, which would account for the fact that Lily Nithercott knows of their cat. Watson and I shall visit them first."

We gave our goodbyes and we followed the map to the Nibleys' home. Their home was found on a branch from the main road we had taken from The Good Lady to the vicarage. It was somewhat larger and marginally better maintained than the average home we had so far seen. It was made of wood that was in sore need of painting. White paint had peeled and flaked in places that showed bare, discoloured wood. A chicken coop stood unsteadily to the right in the back yard with several brown hens scratching behind its fence. A vegetable patch with several rows of plants was located to the left of the yard. A few wooden toys, not all in good repair, cluttered the small porch leading to the door.

Holmes knocked at the entrance.

After several minutes, during which could be heard the sound of children's voices and movement, the door opened. A tall woman, nearly my height, stood before us. Her face seemed washed in tiredness; her hair was limp and uncombed. She held a small child in her left arm, supporting her with her left hip. The child was sucking on three of her fingers. Both were dressed in ill-fitting garments that were faded from washing. The mother looked at us distrustfully.

"Aye?"

Holmes inclined his head respectfully. "Please excuse us for disturbing you, madam. I am Sherlock Holmes, and my companion is Dr. Watson. We are staying at The Good Lady. Mrs. Nithercott requested that we investigate the disappearances of many local animals in the vicinity. I understand that your cat is missing."

"Aye," came the laconic reply. While the name of Mrs. Nithercott had lessened her obvious suspicion, she was still unwelcoming. The sounds of children could be heard, but I could not see them in the dim shadows of the house behind her.

"Would you be able to tell us the circumstances of your cat's disappearance?"

Her reply was slow in coming, and I feared that, perhaps, she had not understood Holmes's question. Finally, she turned her head slightly and yelled with more strength than I would have suspected, "Katie!" She turned back to us. "Katie can tell ye more than me. Fair broke her heart, it did."

A young girl of perhaps thirteen years appeared beside her mother. The resemblance between mother and daughter was striking, but while the mother appeared haggard and worn, her daughter showed all the freshness of youth.

"These men be asking about Blackie," the woman said to her.

Holmes introduced the two of us a second time. "What can you tell us about Blackie, Katie?"

"She's gone missing, sir," said the child in a clear voice devoid of the local pronunciation. "Can you help us find her?"

"I can try. The more you tell me, the more I can help. How did Blackie go missing?"

"I don't know sir. I came down before school. I go to school," she added proudly.

"A right scholar is our Katie," added her mother.

"You came down before school?" prompted Holmes.

"Aye. I set out her milk as always, and I opened the door. Most often, she is at our back door, waiting, but this time she was not there. She sleeps with the chickens. I called for her, but she did not come for it. She does that sometimes."

"So, you weren't alarmed when she didn't appear for her breakfast?"

"No, sir. It be... it is not unusual." I noted again that she was correcting the English of the local dialect, a precision I assumed she had learned in school.

"Did you look for her?

"A little, but I was to get my own breakfast and those of me – my – brothers and sisters while Mum took care of the baby. She was not near the chickens where she sleeps."

"Did Blackie appear while you helped your mother?"

"No sir. Not at all. When I got back from school, her bowl was still full."

"Is that normal?"

"No, sir. I might not see her in the morning, but she always comes later. When that happens, the younger children let her in. Or Mum does."

Her mother said, "She is fair regular. Surprised me, it did, when she didna show at all."

Still addressing Katie, Holmes asked, "Did you look for her then?"

"Yes, sir. I did that. I looked all over." The girl had been composed up until that time, but I saw her lower lip tremble. Vaguely, I wondered how Holmes would handle a crying child, for, to my knowledge, he had little experience with children outside of his Irregulars, all of whom would cut off and arm before permitting tears to be seen. My association with him made me doubtful of his ability to soothe a child, but Katie regained her calm. "I looked everywhere, sir. But I did not find her anywhere. She was gone. We never saw her again."

"I see. You must have been very upset."

"Yes, sir. Very."

"When was this?"

"It were – was – two weeks ago, almost three. It – was on Friday. I remember, sir, for I had thought I would have the weekend with little homework to play with my brothers and sisters, and with Blackie."

Holmes looked at Katie, then at her mother. "Would I be permitted to search your grounds?" Mrs. Nibley seemed unhappily surprised at the request. Distrust appeared in her eyes again, and Holmes continued as if unaware of her reaction, "I have some small skill in reading signs. I might find something that your daughter overlooked."

When Mrs. Nibley hesitated, Katie asked her, "Can he, Mum? It can't be a bad thing, can it?"

She relented. "Aye. I do not know what ye may find after all this time, but ye may look."

"May I watch him?"

Mrs. Nibley considered, and cast another look to Holmes. What she saw must have reassured her somehow. "Stay near the house," she admonished.

"Yes, Mum."

Holmes thanked her graciously, and Mrs. Nibley closed the door.

Katie asked, "What are you going to do?"

Holmes said, "I am going to look. Can you show me where Blackie normally sleeps?"

Katie led us to the chicken coop, which seemed even more precariously built than when seen from afar. She pointed to an area to the left of the building. "This is where."

"Indeed," said Holmes. "I see the depression in the foliage where the grass and flora are not as tall or as dense." And he preceded to bring out his magnifying lens from the pocket of his inverness, crouch to the ground, and examine the area. Slowly, he widened his search. At one point, he made a noise that could have been of astonishment or discovery. After several minutes, he made a similar sound. Katie watched him with big eyes.

Finally, she whispered to me, "What is he doing?"

I whispered back, "He is looking for clues."

"Is he finding any?"

"I do not know," I answered, "but I do know that if there is something to find, Mr. Holmes will find it."

I, who had seen Holmes in action like this many times and had known him to produce astonishing results, was still impressed by the thoroughness and efficiency he had displayed for a case that was, after all, only a missing cat that had probably become prey to another predator.

After more than fifteen minutes had elapsed, he finally stood and looked at us. "Katie," he said.

"Yes, sir."

"Do you put a saucer out for Blackie where she sleeps?"

She seemed almost shocked by the question. "Never, sir! The other animals would get it."

"I see. How often does your father come visit the chickens?"

This time, she was more puzzled than shocked by the question. "Why, again never, sir. He says that keeping the chickens is woman's work."

"Never? He must come here to repair the coop, does he not."

She shook her head. "He has not been here for a very long time. I would know. He works very hard and is tired at the end of the day. It is dark when he is home. And Sunday is the Sabbath."

"I thought as much. Thank you, Katie. Your answers have been both helpful and clear."

She nodded. "Will you be able to find Blackie?"

Holmes paused before answering. "I can only promise to do my best."

"Thank you, sir."

And we took our leave. In silent agreement, we started back to The Good Lady. Twilight was already beginning to fall. Due to the hills surrounding the village, darkness was arriving quicker than in London. Holmes was thoughtful, and I waited until he spoke.

"Odd, Watson."

"What do you mean, Holmes."

"Despite what young Miss Nibley affirmed, I saw a distinct impression of an area dug in the ground as if for a saucer or bowl."

I ventured, "One of the other children placed a bowl there, perhaps?"

"Perhaps. And yet, I saw indications, very faint impressions, of a square-toed boot or shoe of adult size."

"Is that why you asked if her father had been there?"

"Yes."

"Perhaps they are his, and Katie is mistaken."

"Again, perhaps, Watson … though I doubt it. The impressions I saw, tantalizingly partial, indicated a better calibre of footwear than I would expect her father to be able to afford. You saw their house. The sole of the shoe that left these prints was firm and even, with very little wear. I am pressed hard to believe her father's footwear is in such unblemished shape. And I saw other indications, suggestive clues that have been nearly erased by the passage of time and weather, of perhaps three or four other adults, perhaps more, and at least one of them female, present at the same time that those square-toed imprints were made."

"I can conceive of no reason for so many people to be there," I said.

Holmes responded, "I can, and that is what concerns me." And he said nothing more during our return to inn.

Chapter 5

By the time we arrived at the inn, there were perhaps twenty patrons already seated at either the bar or tables. They were men of different types and sizes, but they bore one likeness: they had the look of men for whom life was hard, and work was harder. The younger appeared in the prime of life, strong and virile, and the older appeared craggy and weathered by more than the passage of time. I wondered if those younger men knew that they, too, would look like their elders in twenty years. Those at the bar were drinking ale only, while those at tables were eating meals in addition to partaking of the local brew. The smells were appetizing if not varied, and I was abruptly made aware of how hungry I was.

"Well Watson, let us see what our hostess has for us."

We took our seats at an empty table, and Mrs. Nithercott walked from behind the bar to us. "Mr. Holmes. Dr. Watson. What can I get ye?"

"I cannot speak for Watson, but I believe I see a shepherd's pie accompanied by vegetables at other tables."

"That ye do, Mr. Holmes."

"Then I will take that, with your ale."

I said I would take the same, and she disappeared behind the bar to fetch the order.

"Unusual, isn't it, Watson?"

"What, Holmes?"

"It appears that our host does the cooking, and his wife the socializing."

Our entrance had not gone unremarked. Many of the men pretended to ignore us but would steal occasional glances in our direction. Some looked at us with obvious interest, and others fairly glared at us as if we were intruders which, I suppose, we were.

Holmes murmured, "We are as alien here as if we were in France." And then he added, "Perhaps more so. I suspect the French are more accustomed than these good folks to seeing men from London."

Our hostess arrived with our meal, and I ventured my first bite of shepherd's pie, and the unexpected taste took me by surprise. "Holmes, this is remarkable!"

Holmes, who had already finished his first bite, agreed. "And Watson, assay the vegetables."

They were a common mixture of squash, onion, and sweet pepper, but charred as if cooked over a fire. I tried a pepper, and I found it crisp but hot, and seasoned pleasantly. Seeing my face, Holmes said, smiling at my reaction, "Perhaps men should cook more often."

The ale was both buttery and pleasantly sharp in taste. Mrs. Hudson provided most of our meals in London, and this country meal was up to her standards of excellence. It was certainly better than many a meal I had endured in a London pub. We ate in companionable silence, disturbed only by the inescapable awareness that we were the centre of attention.

The conclusion of our meal left me wondering what there might be for dessert, when I noticed a large man of perhaps forty years step away from the bar and head to our table. He was broad of shoulder, but thick at the waist. His pullover shirt was tan and still stained from the work of the day, and the faded blue vest was only in slightly better shape. He was unshaven with a few day's growth of beard, but I thought his features would not be without appeal to the ladies.

Our hostess noted his movements, and she said, "Dennis, I'll not be expecting any trouble."

He paused and smiled at her, showing missing teeth. "I'll meet that expectation, Aggie."

When he reached our table, he asked, "Is it that I may join ye?" His voice was as rough as his appearance.

"It would be our pleasure," said Holmes, motioning to one of the empty chairs at our table. The man Mrs. Nithercott referred to as "Dennis" sat with a fluid motion. There was an expression in his eye that left no doubt as to why our hostess had admonished him against trouble.

Holmes introduced himself, and then me.

"Dennis Kempthorne," he replied.

"How may Watson and I help you, Mr. Kempthorne?"

"Oh, it be I that can be of help to ye, Mr. Holmes."

Holmes affected puzzlement. "How can you help us?"

"Well, I hear ye be a pretty important person up in London, with books and stories about ye." His tone was a little truculent.

Holmes glanced meaningfully in my direction, and I was forced to recall that he tolerated my literary dabbling with some exasperation. I, for my part, was surprised our interlocuter had become aware of Holmes's reputation in so short of time. While *The Strand* is a widely read publication, I would not have thought that it would have reached this hamlet save for the vicar, and I would have been even more surprised to learn that Kempthorne had read it. Perhaps, Mrs. Nithercott had said something.

"I have had some small successes," responded Holmes, blandly.

"Aye. To look at ye, I would have thought it must be small."

"My good, man!" I ejaculated, but Holmes calmed me.

"Watson, let us remember, we are guests," he murmured. His tone was calm, almost peaceful, but I was not deceived by that. I knew from the way he held his body that that he was ready for any contingency that might arise.

Mrs. Nithercott had been watching the exchange. She came from behind the counter with a firm tread, approached us, put her hands on her hips, and said, scolding, "Dennis Kempthorne! I'll not have ye insulting me guests."

Kempthorne assumed a look of innocence. "Did I insult 'em?" He turned to us. "I do beg yer pardon." The room was silent.

Mrs. Nithercott was unimpressed. "What would yer good mother say if she could see ye?"

Before he could respond, Holmes said, "I am confident that Mr. Kempthorne meant no insult." I was equally confident that the entire room knew better.

Our hostess looked at Holmes, then back to Kempthorne, who said, "Aye. It be as he says. I meant no insult." He turned to Holmes. "No offense."

Holmes replied innocently, "None taken."

With another pair of uneasy glances at both Kempthorne and my friend, Mrs. Nithercott returned to her work behind the counter. The inn was so quiet, the sound of her footsteps echoed like the ring of an axe in the silence.

"Now, my good man, what aid can you provide us?"

"Well, I hear ye be looking for the animals that have gone missing."

"We are indeed."

"I know where they be."

"You surprise me," said Holmes without a trace of surprise in his voice.

Kempthorne motioned expansively. "We all know where they be, don't we lads?" No one said anything, but they watched the exchange intently. I anticipated that some meals would grow cold, so captured were those watching the exchange.

"You would save me and my associate a good deal of time if you were to tell us what you know."

His voice lowered, but I was certain it could still be heard throughout the inn. "The mad monk got 'em, or I miss me guess."

Holmes nodded. "Rev. Clarke mentioned this monk, but he said it was just an old story."

"Aye, so he says. He be too besotted with his book learning to see what be afore his face."

"You believe in this monk, then?"

"Aye. So do we all." He made another expansive gesture, and one or two men nodded. Mrs. Nithercott appeared frozen in place, a glass and towel in hand. Perhaps alerted by the unusual quiet in the room, Mr. Nithercott entered from the door behind the bar. He exchanged a look with his wife, but said nothing.

"Have you seen him?"

"The monk? Of course not! No one sees him. But we see the lights."

"Lights?"

"Aye. Lights of odd colours every Friday night, up in the ruins." More men nodded. "But don't believe me, ask Arley."

One of the men in front of the bar, spoke. He was younger than Kempthorne by perhaps a decade. "Dennis speaks truth," he declared stoutly. "I seen 'em when out hunting at night. There be lights as blue as the sky, or red like fire, or orange as a pumpkin."

A third man at one of the tables added, "I saw green lights. Gave me the willies, it did."

"Allus at the Abbey," came another voice.

Another said, "Sometimes there be shadows."

"Me wife has seen 'em."

Holmes said, "At what time of night does this happen? Early evening?"

Kempthorne shook his head with a wicked gleam in his eye. "Nay. More like midnight, though it be hard to tell."

More men nodded and voiced their assent. "Sometimes it be as early as eleven or as late as one."

Holmes looked around. "Have you all seen these lights?"

Some gave their assent, but others shook their heads. "They come and go."

"Do you see them only on Friday nights?"

This gave everyone pause. Finally, an older man said, "Aye. Only on Friday, but there be weeks between 'em sometimes."

"Has anyone gone to investigate?"

The looks from the spectators made it quite clear that none would dare visit the abbey, and further, they considered it unthinkable that anyone would even suggest it. A younger man said, "No one goes there."

Holmes seemed to give this information deep thought. "I see. Mr. Kempthorne, this is important information indeed." He turned to our hosts. "Would it be possible to inform young Mr. Symes that we would be happy to hire his services tomorrow?"

Mr. Nithercott said, warily, "Aye. I can give him that message. He like to be not ready afore the afternoon. He must help his parents."

"Understood. That would be acceptable. Watson and I have plans for the morning."

I wondered what those plans might be, but said nothing. Holmes would certainly tell me when he had opportunity.

"Where be ye going, Mr. Holmes?" Mr. Nithercott asked. "Be ye returning to London already?"

"By no means. Watson and I intend to pay a visit to the abbey."

A gasp of astonishment circled the room. Mrs. Nithercott said, "Surely not!"

"Surely yes," Holmes contradicted.

"But the mad monk!"

Holmes smiled. "But he is only abroad at night, am I right?"

There was a hesitant murmur of agreement.

"And Watson and I will visit during the day. We shall be quite safe, won't we Watson?"

"Assuredly," I agreed.

Kempthorne shook his head. "This be very foolhardy, I be thinking." He shook his head again. All his veiled, hostile manner had changed to one of grudging respect. "Perhaps ye in London don't hold stock with the mad monk, but there be more things than ye know."

Holmes smiled at what we both recognized was an unconscious quote of the Bard of Stratford-upon-Avon. "Of that, I am as certain as you."

Chapter 6

We broke our fast the next day on a delightful mixture of eggs, bread, cheese, and bacon that was drizzled delicately in a mild sauce that only enhanced its flavour. The ale with which we washed it down was a golden brew that left a nutty taste behind it. I could recall French wines that had given me less pleasure.

We were the only inhabitants of the inn that morning, and I supposed that the bulk of their business was during the evening hours. When we finished, Holmes said to Mrs. Nithercott, "Please, give our compliments to your husband. This meal, and last night's, have been some of the best food I have ever consumed."

"Holmes is correct," I agreed. "Had I not experienced it myself, I would not have credited it. I have eaten meals in some of the best hotels in London that were not as good."

Our hostess smiled broadly at us. "Ivor will be pleased to hear ye say so. It were his father who taught him, and who owned the inn afore us."

"Your husband," said Holmes, "could make a living anywhere with such skills."

She shook her head. "He will never leave Wenlock Edge, and neither would I want to. We be known here, and it suits us. But I'll tell him what ye've said."

She turned to her work, but she could not quite hide her pleased, proud smile before she left us.

"Well, Watson, I have been giving our day some thought."

"As have I."

"Before we visit the mysterious Waltham Abbey this afternoon, I thought to pay a call on each of those who have experienced the loss of a pet or livestock."

Before we could continue the conversation, Lily Nithercott entered the room from the door behind the bar, carrying a doll made of porcelain that was rather finely dressed. It seemed a surprising mark of wealth in this town, and I suspected no little sacrifice had gone into its purchase by her parents. It was another sign of how they doted on their daughter.

She made a bee-line to me. "Me dolly be feeling poorly," she declared. "Ye said ye would help her."

Before I could speak, her mother intervened. "Lily, I be certain that Dr. Watson has other plans for his day."

Holmes also intervened. "He does, but, as I was about to propose that Dr. Watson and I split our investigation, he may have time for both."

Looking at the little girl, I said, genuinely, "Nothing could please me more." She rewarded me with a bright smile.

"Watson, I will pay a call on the Morely's and visit the Gresham and Bradshaw farms. The three are in close proximity, and I should like to test a theory. If you would be willing to visit Mr. Kent and enquire concerning the loss of his terrier, Alexander, we should both be able to return in sufficient time to compare our findings and meet young Joseph Symes for our trip to the abbey."

He passed me the rough map that Jeremiah Clarke and his wife had drafted for us. "Shouldn't you keep this, Holmes?"

"Having had it in my possession last night, I have memorized it," he informed me.

Lily looked at Holmes. "Have ye found Blackie, yet?"

"No," Holmes told her, and then he paused. I could see an uncomfortable shadow pass his face. I suspected that he, like I, considered it unlikely that the young child would see Blackie again. The cat had been too long missing, especially if Holmes was correct in his suspicions that human agency was involved. He was no doubt considering how to prepare Lily for that eventuality.

It thought it best that I postpone the conversation. "Perhaps, Holmes, it would be best if you started now. You have three homes to investigate to my one, after all."

Holmes rallied, and I thought he appeared a little relieved. "Indeed, Watson. I shall meet you here on my return." And he exited the inn.

I turned my attention to the little girl. "So, what seems to be your dolly's problem?"

Seriously, she answered, "She be coughing somat often. I be worried that her lungs be weak."

I composed my face into one that was equally serious. "Then you must let me fetch my bag."

None of this had escaped her mother's notice. As I headed for the stairs to obtain my room, she looked gratefully to me. It was a moment's work to fetch my bag and return to the main room. Lily was waiting patiently for my return. I sat in the chair in front of her and extracted my stethoscope from my bag.

"Tell me, what is your dolly's name."

"Dolly."

"Ah. Well, Dolly, may I examine your lungs?"

Lily answered for her. "She doesna want to. She be scared."

I smiled. "There is no reason to be frightened. I promise you and Dolly that it won't hurt."

Lily held her doll up to me, so incongruously dressed in finery that I would have expected to see only in a ballroom, and I touched the diaphragm to the doll's chest. I pretended to listen intently. I moved the diaphragm to another part of its chest and listened again. I nodded sagely, then put my stethoscope away and turned to Lily.

"I am pleased to tell you that Dolly only has a small cold."

"Be that good?"

"It is very good. It is nothing serious."

"I be afeared she had newmona." At first, I did not understand what she said, but then assumed that she meant pneumonia.

"That would be very bad, but she doesn't have anything so serious. I have heard no water in her lungs."

"Can ye give her somat that will make her feel better?"

Thankful that I had thought to bring my medical satchel and my most frequent medications, including the one I employed when faced with those patients who had no valid illness but merely sundry complaints that only needed a dollop of sympathy, I said, "I can indeed." I pulled out the paper envelope in which I kept starch that

I coloured with marigold petals and flavoured with a small amount of pepper. "Do you have a small cup?"

She immediately went to her mother, who reached under the counter and gave her a glass. Lily returned to me. Very carefully, I poured a small amount of the coloured starch into the glass.

"You must be very careful with this. Mix a small amount with water so it becomes a paste, and put the result on her chest before bed for the next three days. Do not put too much, as it is very potent. Just a little. In three days, she will be much better."

Lily suddenly beamed at me. "Thank ye, Dr. Watson."

"You are greatly welcome."

Mrs. Nithercott seemed nearly as pleased as her daughter. Lily began to skip to exit the way she had entered, but stopped suddenly before she disappeared behind the counter. She turned back to me, her face suddenly changed. She walked back and whispered to me conspiratorially, "Ye know, Dolly really be not real."

I whispered back. "Neither was the powder I gave you."

She beamed again, and this time, glass in hand, she skipped behind the counter and through the open door to what I presumed was the kitchen. Mrs. Nithercott was smiling at me fondly.

"Thank ye, Doctor, for yer kindness. Ivor and I, we be proud of Lily."

"You should be. She is a delightful child."

"Perhaps we spoil her."

"I am of the firm opinion that children need spoiling."

"And ye be so good with her. Ye will be a good father."

"I hope to be." And then I asked, "How had she heard about pneumonia?"

Her face darkened. "Last year, Lily had it. She were only four, but she remembers it."

I nodded. "That must have been very worrying."

"It were that, it were. She were very sick. Ivor and I, we be very frightened. And then she shook herself out of the memory. "That be last year. This year be better."

"I am gratified to hear it."

"She be strong and happy now." I could see the signs of strong emotion in her face. "It was so long. We never thought to have a child." And then she said, "Excuse me," and left me alone in the room. I could only think that she and her husband deserved the happiness that an unexpected child could bring. Their love and devotion for their daughter was obvious for even the most illiterate to read.

My fictional examination and diagnosis completed, I returned my bag to my room. Then, with map in hand, I started on the assignment Holmes had given me. Kirby Kent's residence was a short distance away from The Good Lady, and the walk provided another opportunity to assess the town and its populace. Those I passed nodded politely, and I began to realize that, despite my first impression, while the wealth of London was far removed, most of the people I passed seemed to have sufficient food and clothing to be content with their lot. While I missed the teeming bustle of London, I began to appreciate the quiet, more sedate pace of village life, where the roads appeared built primarily for pedestrians rather than carriages. Although our stated reason for visiting Wenlock Edge – rest and relaxation – was pure invention, perhaps it would be more accurate than we had anticipated.

But at the same time, I was conscious of a common look of unease in many whom I chanced to pass. I would catch a woman with children walking more quickly than was natural, and the mother would cast an occasional anxious glance in the direction of the abbey, which could be seen between houses depending on their angle and the space between them. I could well understand Rev. Clarke's concern for his parishioners. There was worry, perhaps even fear, in some of the glances.

As I had yesterday with Holmes, I left the closely packed buildings of the main village behind and was soon among homes farther apart. The home of Kirby Kent, whose dog Alexander had gone missing, was typical. It was a one-storey cottage with an unsteady porch, shingled by grey slate and framed in rough wood. The lawn was surrounded on three sides by a hedge of untended yew. The grass would soon be in need of trimming. All in all, it presented to the visitor an impression of the same, almost universal neglect that I had noted the day before in other homes.

I knocked on the door and almost immediately heard the shuffle of slow movement. It took more time than I would have thought required for a home so small, but the door eventually opened, and I was able to see an elderly man as neglected as his yard. His face was unshaven; his hair sparse and uncombed. He had the rheumy look of age, and the sallow complexion of a man not often in the sun. Thin, almost emaciated, his clothing hung on him as if attempting to pull him to the ground by its weight. I wondered if he was eating regularly, and I regretted leaving my medical satchel at the inn. His stance was as unsteady as his porch, and he looked at me without recognition. His mouth moved as if he was attempting to remember who I was.

I introduced myself, and immediately, a light glimmered in his eyes.

"Aye," he said. "Ye be the detective from London."

"No," I replied, wondering how he had heard of Holmes. "That would be my companion, Sherlock Holmes. He is a consulting detective. I am a doctor and his friend."

He nodded. "Come in. I get few visitors outside of me son."

As I entered the home, I was struck by the disarray of discarded clothing, plates that had not yet been removed and cleaned, and furniture that had seen better days.

"Ye'll have to forgive the mess. Since me Peggy passed on, I've not been able to keep it up. A right neat one, she were." And then he added, "Though I were better when Alexander were here."

He moved some clothing off of a chair for me, and I sat carefully. "Alexander was your dog?"

"Aye." He moved slowly to another chair, obviously his favourite, and sat. I wondered that he could endure the walk to The Good Lady. "He were a good dog. More like a person. Allus with me. Kept me young." His mouth trembled. "I miss him terrible. Almost as much as me Peggy."

"I am so sorry. When did your wife die?"

He considered. "More'n two years past. We be married 51 years."

"That is a wonderful testimony to the institution of marriage!"

He regarded me keenly. "Be ye married?"

"I am engaged and hope to be married this December."

"Aye. Thought as much. A handsome feller like ye be. Treat'er well, and she'll treat ye well."

"I have every intention of taking your advice. She's a wonderful woman." I let a polite pause interrupt our conversation before asking, "Since you know that my friend is a detective, did you know that the Nithercotts have requested that we investigate the disappearance of your animal?"

"Aye, but Alexander weren't no animal. Like a person he were. One of the family."

"I understand. When did he ... disappear?"

He barely needed to think about it. "T'were Thursday a month afore now. Late. We be gone to the inn, you see, he and I. Ivor, he be a good cook. Even me Peggy said so, and we would eat there, we three, ever' Friday. Sometimes the food were odd, but it allus were good."

"And you and Alexander continued those visits to the inn every Friday after your wife passed?"

"Aye. Sometimes more often. I have savings, ye see. Me Peggy, she were a saver."

"When did you notice that Alexander was gone?"

"We had gotten home. It were dark. When we got home, Alexander barked and growled. I thought, 'He's heard somat, perhaps a hare.' It be allus good for a dog to chase the hare, though they never catch 'em."

"No doubt."

"So, I said, 'Go get 'im, boy. Give 'im one for me.' Off he went. He done it afore. A little exercise afore bed. But that time, he didna come in when I called. And I called and called."

"Had you gone in without him?"

"Aye. Thought he might be a while. But I called and called. He never said a word."

"Did you see the… hare?"

"Nay. Me eyes be not so good in the dark now."

"Did you see anything at all?"

"Nay." His mouth quivered. "He just never came back. And I called and called." He was visibly troubled at the memory, and I recognized that I was upsetting him.

"Did you hear something perhaps? A struggle between animals?"

"Nay. Me hearing be not so good now."

I was at a loss for another question to ask, and I keenly felt the anxious thought that I was letting Holmes down. I could not see how any of the information, most of it an absence of information, would do our investigation any good.

"I called and called," he informed me yet again.

"I'm sure you did, Mr. Kent. You did everything you could have done."

"I dinna believe he run off."

I found myself saying, "Neither do I," though I could not possibly have been certain. I was full of pity for the man.

"Somat's happened to him. I called and called, and he didna come."

I considered this my opportunity. "That's why I'm here. I can't promise I will find something, but I wonder if I might look in your yard. Perhaps I will find some indication of what happened."

His mouth moved soundlessly before he said, "But ye dinna think ye'll find somat, do ye?"

"I can't promise anything. I can only try."

Eventually, he gave me permission, perhaps because our interview had tired him and he wanted to rest. I left him sitting in his room. I was convinced that his pet was the reason he continued to live after his wife's death, and I worried that he was declining quickly without that reason to go on living. I resolved to exert myself to the utmost to find a clue.

But I found the fulfilment of that resolve more difficult than the promise. I attempted to emulate Holmes and his minute examination of the premises, but I felt rather foolish crouching on my knees, peering at the grass and examining the yew bushes and yet finding nothing at all. The latter had several small gaps, but I could draw no conclusions from them other than the obvious: a small dog could exit through them. But why would the dog do that? It had lived with his master for years. I could conceive of no reason why it would leave the yard or, upon leaving, fail to return unless it found another animal that was hungry, larger, and more vicious. I looked for footprints, but I saw nothing.

After a fruitless half hour, more perhaps, I rose to my feet, not without some discomfort from the wounds I had incurred in the course of my military duty. I had failed to find anything that would help my friend resolve the disappearances, and I had nothing to offer Mr. Kent.

As we had arranged, I returned to the inn to wait for Holmes. We expected Joseph Symes with his cart at three o'clock. I had a late lunch of rabbit in a delicate sauce, with potatoes and turnips. Mrs. Nithercott informed me that it would be served that evening for dinner, but it wouldn't hurt for me to have an advance on that meal.

Holmes joined me in the common room of the inn at two. With a tact worthy of Mrs. Hudson, Mrs. Nithercott left the common room through the door behind the bar, leaving the room to Holmes and me. Immediately, I recognized in him the excitement of the hunt, and I knew he had found something. He sat down, and without preamble asked, "What did you learn?"

"Very little Holmes, and I fear nothing that will help."

"Perhaps not. We shall see, for my recent investigations have uncovered a pattern for which I have no explanation as yet. Tell me, did Mr. Kent's canine companion disappear on Thursday night or Friday morning four weeks ago?"

I was surprised. "Why, yes! How did you know?"

"Because it fits the pattern, Watson. In fact, as my investigation uncovered the pattern, I returned and spoke to Mrs.

Nibley and her daughter, Katie, again. Then I returned to the first domiciles I visited. Human memory is unreliable, but making allowances for that, there was a clear pattern to the disappearances."

"What was it?"

"This: each disappearance was noticed either Thursday night or sometime during the following day, generally but not always in the morning."

"Holmes, no animal would be so regular!"

"You have struck to the heart of the matter, Watson. Had we not already suspected human agency in these disappearances, the regularity of the missing animals would suggest it. Moreover, in three of the disappearances – four altogether counting the Nibley home – I found indications, faint ones, of multiple footprints for which I cannot account. The ground around the Gresham pigsty was particularly soft, and I found several good prints that could not be explained by examining the footwear of the family. One of those imprints was a square-toed boot belonging to a man whom I estimate from the stride and depth of the impressions to be over six feet tall, but slender."

"Holmes, are you saying that not only are people responsible for this rash of disappearances, but the same people are involved?"

"It is not yet certain, but I consider it more than likely." Holmes's face hardened. "But there is more."

"More? This is already hard to credit."

"The first disappearance was the Nibleys' cat. If your information from Mr. Kent is correct, his terrier was next."

"I was unable to find any indication of foul play."

Holmes dismissed the admission with a wave of his hand. "That is no matter. It is understandable that the passage of time would eradicate all traces that existed." I was well aware that Holmes had found clues at the Nibleys' chicken coop, and if his theory was correct, that was an entire week before Mr. Kent's dog vanished. I said nothing, but I once again felt that I had let my friend down.

But Holmes continued. "The next was a spaniel at the Morley home, missed on Friday morning when the owners noticed that it had not eaten the table scraps left for it on the back porch. The Bradshaws noticed they were short a piglet only on Friday afternoon, perhaps because they assumed all the piglets were there when they fed the pigs in the morning. Finally, the Gresham girls noticed that the kid was gone early Friday morning, for they intended to treat it like a baby and dress it in one of their old bonnets. Do you see the pattern, Watson?"

"Other than what you already explained, that the animals likely disappeared on the same day of the week, Thursday, and during the night, no."

"Ah, Watson, you disappoint me; I thought it obvious. But perhaps I do you an injustice. You are not a veterinarian, and you had no opportunity to interview all the families as I have, save Mr. Kent. Watson, each animal taken was bigger than the last, almost as if the abductors are working their way up the animal kingdom."

I was bewildered. "But, why?"

"I do not know."

"Could it be some kind of bizarre feud between local families? Each one increasing the feud by taking a larger animal?"

Holmes shook his head. "It is possible, but I can find no known animosity between these families."

"I can see no sense in any of this."

"Nor can I. It cannot be nonsensical, for there is a pattern, but I can find no logical motive to account for the pattern."

"Could it be the work of a madman?"

Holmes shook his head. "I saw indications of at least four different people involved, and I suspect there were more. Unless there is a form of contagious insanity of which I am unaware, I am hard pressed to deduce so many men and women are hiding a madness of this nature and that it has gone unremarked for so long in this insular village. No, Watson, there is something here I am missing."

"Holmes, you frighten me."

He looked at me. "Old boy, there is no need to give way to fear. There is only something, perhaps many things, that remain unknown."

"How will we uncover them?"

Before Holmes could respond, Mrs. Nithercott entered the common room. "Young master Symes be here," she informed us almost at the same time as the red-haired young man entered the inn from outside.

"As arranged, our next step," Holmes told me, "will be to visit Waltham Abbey and determine if the home of the mad monk can shed some light on our little problem."

Chapter 7

Waltham Abbey was at the end of a long, winding, steep road of compressed dirt, somewhat overgrown by foliage and encroached upon by the surrounding forest. At times, a low-hanging tree branch would brush our heads. The fact that the road could still be used at all after all these centuries was an indication of how often it had been used when the abbey had served as a monastery of the Roman Catholic religion. Remembering my history, I recalled that the decline of the papistry in England first began in the 1500s under Henry VIII and continued under Elizabeth I after her struggle with Mary, Queen of Scots. The establishment of the Church of England meant the disestablishment of many if not all Roman Catholic monasteries in 1532. Since then, the road would have been unused, except by the curious, for over two and a half centuries. It was a testament to the thoroughness of its original construction.

Joseph Symes remained talkative through the ride, and it prompted Holmes to remark, "Mr. Symes, you do not seem to be at all concerned with the prospect of visiting the Abbey. Many of your fellow townsmen appear frightened of it."

"Aye. That be true."

"May I enquire as to why?"

"Well, the curate, he says good Christian folks should not be afeared of ghosts and witches, and mayhap they don't exist anyways." And he added, "Better to fear God, says he, and be kind to our neighbours."

I thought that Rev. Clarke would be pleased to learn that one of his parishioners, at least, had adopted his views on the topic.

"You surprise me. Many people believe the curate to be wrong on this issue. Have you heard about the lights?"

"Aye, that I have."

"But you aren't afraid of them."

He glanced at Holmes and said, with a smile, "They be but lights."

Holmes nodded. "A refreshingly reasonable position. Have you actually seen them?"

He sobered. "Oncet. I and some of me friends were out late for a few pints. It were Teddy who saw 'em first. 'Look', says he, 'it be the mad monk!' I saw them then. They be red, then blue. There be weird shadows."

"And you were unafraid?"

The young man paused before answering. "Well, truth be, it were an odd sight, and that be no lie. I were a little queasy, and glad I were in town and not up at the abbey."

"And now?"

He grinned at us again. "It be day and the sun be out."

Holmes smiled back. "Just so. Have you ever been here before?"

At this, our guide actually blushed. "Aye. Some of me friends dared me. I were just a little thing. But then, there be no lights then."

I could tell that Symes's last statement interested Holmes. "Indeed! So, the lights are a new phenomenon?"

Symes seemed puzzled, and I suspected the young man didn't understand the word "phenomenon." I said, "Mr. Holmes means that no one had seen lights at the abbey previously."

He nodded. "Aye. It be a new thing."

Holmes asked, "When did they begin?"

"It be hard to say. Not so long ago." He considered the question. "A year, mayhap?"

"So, before pets and farm animals began disappearing."

"Oh, aye! Long afore that."

Eventually, we arrived at the abbey. In its prime, it must have been an awe-inspiring sight, with high, stone walls, above which peeked the even higher towers of the church and other edifices in the abbey. The road led to a gate, whose broad, double doors had long ago collapsed from disuse and age, one leaning precariously by hand-crafted, rusted hinges. The door was lacking many of its planks. Entering the abbey, now partially overgrown with creeping weeds, ivy, and juniper, I could see the lower buildings that I thought were perhaps dormitories. There was a large building that appeared to have once been a stable. Beside it were the remains of several animal pens, now completely overgrown and whose fences were merely suggested by fallen wood, now rotted. They would never contain livestock again. Here, in the main square of the dilapidated abbey, I was struck not by awe, but by a feeling of dread, almost animosity.

A hare was on the edge of the square as we entered. It paused to examine us, its nose twitching, before it scampered off into the vegetation.

By far, the largest structure was the church. It retained only the bare skeletons of its former glory. It was several storeys tall. I could see five large windows on the side facing us. Fingers of the leading suggesting the pattern of the windows that had once supported stained glass. The glass in the windows, and some of the lead, was completely gone. The effect was rather like the branches of a tree whose leaves had already fallen in preparation for a bitter winter. A heap of man-made and natural detritus that had blown or fallen against the door blocked entry to the church itself. The atmosphere was not merely one of abandonment, but one of melancholy, perhaps despair. I shivered, and not from the cold. Our guide had also become silent.

Holmes, as usual, was completely unaffected by such impressions. He fairly leapt from his seat beside Symes and strode fearlessly to the church building. His head moved constantly as he swept the ground with his eyes. I followed him less easily, as the cool weather and inactivity from the long ride had stiffened the wounds I had received in the war. Symes remained seated on the cart for a moment, then dismounted and began brushing the horses, talking to them in a low voice. He made no move to join us.

As I approached Holmes, I could feel under my feet and then hear the crunching of glass that I presumed had fallen from the windows.

Holmes looked at me. "I would have thought that the original inhabitants would have removed anything of value from the monastery upon their departure, including the stained-glass work that must have been beautiful and striking during its day. But it would appear that the panes remained in the windows until brought down by the passage of time."

"Perhaps they were too difficult to remove."

"I have no doubt you are correct, Watson."

Holmes began a thorough examination of the wall, now infested with creeping ivy, even removing his magnifying glass and examining it slowly. After a time, he turned his attention to the ground in front of it. I glanced at the sun, which was declining in the sky, and my action didn't escape Holmes's notice.

"Yes, Watson, there is insufficient time for a meticulous examination before nightfall makes the return trip unsafe."

"There are too many buildings to examine them all."

"Then we shall concentrate our efforts on the only building that has been recently used: the church."

I was perplexed. "The church? But the door is blocked! The church is completely inaccessible!"

Holmes glanced at me. "No, Watson, that was what we were meant to think."

"But, Holmes...."

"Follow me, Watson." He took me around to the front of the edifice. I looked back at Joseph Symes, but he had moved the horses and cart under the shade of a tree and could no longer be seen. Holmes pointed. "The ground leading up to the church shows the unmistakable signs of the tread of men other than ourselves, while the grass and flora farther away from the church is untrodden." I looked around but saw nothing. Holmes must have read my scepticism on my face, for he motioned me to follow him. He led me to the barred doorway of the church. "What do you see, Watson?"

"I see tree branches, logs, and beams that have fallen in front of the front doors, which are now overgrown with creeping vines and other plants."

"But Watson, how did those branches and beams arrive at their place?"

"They fell?" I suggested.

"From where, Watson, from where?"

And then I realized what my friend had already deduced. There were no trees close enough to account for so many limbs to have fallen in front of the door. Some of the branches were bigger than I was. Certainly, no wind could have blown limbs of that size so far from the trees in the abbey holding. The other ruined buildings were too far away to account for the beams that were there.

Holmes continued, "But if that alone does not convince you, look closer at the wood. There are nails in the wood holding pieces together, nails that were never used by the monks who built these buildings for the simple reason that such nails did not exist in their day. Examine the twine holding limbs and beams together. While showing signs of exposure to the elements, the twine is new. This barrier was purposefully built."

"Why would someone do that?"

"To make it look as if no one could possibly enter the church without significant work, and yet make it easy to do so for those who knew better. With your help, I will demonstrate. Grasp the beam to your left," my friend said pointing. Then he walked purposefully to the other end and readied himself. "Now, lift."

To my surprise, the entire jumble of rubbish lifted easily away from the door of the church. Holmes swung his end around and we laid it against the wall. I was impressed by the ingenious method. To me, it had appeared a serious deterrent to entry, and yet it took hardly any effort or time to accomplish. I was even more amazed, not for the first time, by Holmes's perspicacity and observational powers. To me, it had appeared an insurmountable barrier.

"Now, let us see what someone wished to remain hidden."

We entered first into the vestibule and then the main sanctuary. I noted that the windows on the other side of the building were as devoid of glass as the side I first saw upon entry to the abbey grounds. Even here inside, ivy and other plants were growing. To my surprise, there were no pews, not even the remnants of pews. Reading my thoughts again, Holmes remarked, "I would expect that they were removed for the wood by the townspeople centuries ago before tales of the mad monk made such a trip less tempting for the superstitious."

We approached the raised platform where an ornate, stone altar still stood. The church itself was built in the shape of a cross and was a remarkable feat of engineering, especially considering that it must have been raised by hand in the eleventh century, or perhaps earlier, when there was no machinery to make construction easier. As we moved slowly through the collection of dirt and dust that witnessed to the accumulation of centuries, I received a rude shock.

"Holmes! Bones!"

"I see them, Watson."

In front of the level spot before the altar, laid out in a large circle, were five piles of bones, equidistant from each other. Holmes knelt down before one of the smaller piles and began separating them. "A cat, I believe, Watson." I too, bent down to separate bones in another pile. Fetal pigs are often used in medical school because of the similarity to human physiology, and I was certain I was looking at the remains of the Bradshaw piglet. As we examined each pile, we were forced to conclude that we had found the missing creatures.

"Holmes, no animal did this."

"Agreed, Watson. If we could not already deduce the handiwork of human beings from the blocked doorway, this indisputably confirms that the disappearances are the work of one or more men." He had already extracted his magnifying glass from his inverness, and he was examining the ground around the piles. I watched as he moved slowly from spot to spot. The area in the church darkened as the sun set, and the shadows lengthened and deepened in the building.

After a long time, Holmes straightened. "I can do no more at the present. At least ten different footprints, perhaps as many as a dozen. There have been many people here, often, and not long ago. Our square-toed friend was among their number." He made a noise of disgust. "I should have had the foresight to bring a lantern." He regained his good humour and cast a mischievous look in my direction. "Should you decide to chronicle this adventure for the public as you did the affair that began on Brixton Road, do not fail to mention the oversight. It will be certain to reduce the aura of near infallibility with which you have seen fit to imbue me in your chronicles." He chuckled and I followed him out of the church, and he shut the door behind us.

"Help me replace the barrier, Watson. I do not want to advertise the fact that we have been inside. Someone left the pile of bones there for a reason. I do not want it known that we have discovered them."

I helped Holmes place the barrier back where it had been, and we walked away from the church and our gruesome discovery. Before we reached the cart, where Symes was waiting, Holmes gripped my arm. "No word of this to our young friend. There is enough fear among the village without idle gossipers discussing piles of bones and speculating on the reasons they have been placed there."

"Do you know the reason, Holmes?"

He hesitated. "One theory comes to mind, but it is a fantastic explanation, and probably as fanciful as it is alarming. I will not subject you to it." He released my arm and approached the cart.

"Did ye find somat, Mr. Holmes?" asked our young conductor. Having heard us, he moved around to the front of the cart. "Ye spent a goodly time."

Given his admonition to me, I wondered how Holmes would answer. He decided to speak truthfully, but vaguely. "Indications only, Mr. Symes. I found indications, but they need to be considered before drawing any conclusions."

The young man nodded as if he understood and was in agreement. "Then it be good we be going. The dark will be on us afore we reach Wenlock Edge." The three of us climbed onto the seat of the cart, and Symes turned it around to head back to the village. I could not help but glance back at the church with its macabre findings. Silhouetted by the setting sun, it seemed more menacing than before, more likely to house the unhappy ghost of a mad monk walking its grounds in search of the unwary.

As our guide predicted, it was dark before we reached the village. As if by agreement, the three of us had been silent as we travelled in the growing darkness as we each tended to his own thoughts. I suspected Holmes was considering our unexpected discovery before the abandoned altar. I, too, wondered what the piles of bones might mean, but I also pondered on Holmes's unspoken theory. For my part, I could concoct no conjecture that would explain stealing animals, killing them, and then placing their bones in piles, other than some form of madness. The bones had been devoid of sinew and flesh, indicating to me that they had been cooked clean. I shuddered at such a gruesome thought. What possible motivation could there be for such a grisly action?

Our guide brought us to the door of The Good Lady, and Holmes provided another generous tip in addition to his fee. "Thankee, Mr. Holmes. Just ask if ye need me again."

"You may be certain of it, Mr. Symes."

I had thought the evening would hold no more surprises for us, but I was wrong. It was the dinner hour, and the common room was busy, with men, and some women, eating meals or drinking ale. That was expected, of course. What was unexpected was our hostess' reaction on seeing us. She immediately excused herself from a conversation with one of her customers, and met us before we could ascend the stairs to our rooms. She was visibly agitated. When she spoke, her voice was lowered.

"I beg pardon, Mr. Holmes. Dr. Watson. But ye have a visitor."

"Indeed," said Holmes, his eyebrow raised in mild surprise. "The vicar, perhaps? I had complimented him on his library."

"Nay. It be Lord Arbury hisself. He has never been here afore today."

"How unusual!" stated Holmes, mildly. "Did he state his business?"

"Nay. He demanded to speak with ye at once. When I told him ye were out, he asked where ye were."

"Did you tell him?"

"I did that. I didna think anything of it. I told him ye were at the abbey, and he were wroth." The good woman was fearful and anxious. "I do hope I do nothing wrong."

Holmes immediately did what he could to calm her. "Of course you have done nothing wrong! He asked where we were, and you told him. What could possibly be wrong with that?"

"I dinna know Mr. Holmes, but he were so angry! I be glad there be others here." She nodded to those gathered in the common room who, while they could not possibly hear us, were watching us closely. Those that had been here when Lord Arbury entered certainly suspected the topic of conversation. "I were afeared he would strike me." And the poor woman trembled at the thought. "He be such an important man."

Holmes's expression changed to one of controlled anger. "I think very little of a man, no matter how supposedly important, who would frighten a woman so badly she feared violence."

"I will add my agreement to that," I said. "It is churlish and ungentlemanly in the extreme."

Mrs. Nithercott put a hand to her chest. Her eyes filled with unshed tears. "Thank ye, both. I truly be frightened. Ivor, he be in the kitchen, or even Lord Arbury wouldna dared." Remembering Mr. Nithercott's stout physique, I decided she was correct.

"Where is Lord Arbury now?" asked Holmes.

She inadvertently glanced at the stairs. "In the last room, Mr. Holmes, beside Dr. Watson's room. He were set on staying until ye returned from the abbey."

"One last question: when was all this?"

"Oh, Mr. Holmes! Nearly two hours past!"

"Two hours? His errand must be pressing indeed if he was willing to wait for us as long as that." And then he added, "Think no more of it, Mrs. Nithercott, and return to your guests. We'll be down after our conversation with Lord Arbury to partake of more of your husband's inventive cooking."

Realizing that all eyes were on us, some frankly and some surreptitiously, she collected herself, smiled at us, thanked us both, and returned to her place behind the bar.

As we started up the stairs, Holmes said, "This is unexpected and should prove interesting."

I could only agree.

Reaching the room indicated by Mrs. Nithercott, Holmes knocked on the closed door. "Enter," came a commanding voice, and we obeyed.

Lord Arbury stood between the bed and the window and had turned to face us upon our entry. He was a tall man, but ascetically thin, almost cadaverous in his appearance. His face was pale and the skin thinly stretched over his skull. Except for a fringe of grey hair over his ears that circled back around his head, he was completely bald. His eyes were a striking blue, but they were without warmth or human feeling. He was dressed immaculately, in a dark grey suit and matching vest, a white shirt with a high collar, and a black cravat held in place by a gold bar.

"You have kept me waiting, Mr. Holmes." His tone was cruel and condescending.

"No doubt," returned Holmes, coldly. "Had you called ahead and not arrived unannounced, perhaps we could have arranged our day to meet you either here or at Arbury Hall at our mutual convenience."

Arbury flushed with anger at Holmes's manner. "Do you know who I am, Mr. Holmes?" he retorted.

"Outside of your title, no, nor do I care. I am unimpressed by titles. Do you know who I am, Lord Arbury?"

He made a noise of derision. "A self-important mountebank who fancies himself an investigator."

"I prefer the title, 'consulting detective.'"

"No doubt you do. A pretentious title to impress the credulous and dissemble your own lack of reputation."

Holmes smiled thinly. "If my reputation is so lacking, then why are you here, Lord Arbury?"

He flushed again. "To prevent your meddling and the harm you seem intent on doing." He seemed to take notice of me for the first time. "Have your man leave. We have something to discuss."

"Watson stays, or this conversation will end now."

The two locked eyes. Neither appeared willing to accede to the other.

"Holmes," I began, "I can retire to my room while you speak with Lord Arbury."

"You will do nothing of the sort, Watson. If Lord Arbury is unwilling to speak with both of us, then he can return to his home unsatisfied." After a pause, he added, "I suspect I will sleep adequately tonight no matter what decision he makes."

There was a flash of anger in our visitor's eyes that I had seen in few men, and I realized why our hostess had been so upset by him. Without leaving his side, his hand twitched as if he would strike Holmes. Holmes feigned to be unperturbed.

"Well, Lord Arbury? Watson and I have not yet eaten our evening meal. Speak or leave. I am not overly concerned with your decision, only that it is made."

"I am not accustomed to being treated in such a high-handed manner, Mr. Holmes." There was an unspoken threat behind his words.

"Based upon our short acquaintance, I consider your exposure to such an experience long overdue."

"You will rue this treatment."

"I think not. Well? Speak or leave."

After a moment, he said, "Your presence is not wanted here, Mr. Holmes. I understand you have been ferreting about the abandoned abbey, which is an unwarranted intrusion to the ghosts of those who built it. You are only stirring up trouble where none exists. I suggest you and your... associate... pack your bags and take the next train back to London. I have taken the liberty of enquiring, and I have determined that the next train will arrive at a quarter to nine tomorrow."

"My investigation is not yet complete."

"Complete it."

"I anticipate that it will take several more days to bring the investigation to a successful conclusion, perhaps more."

His hand moved as before. Though it again did not leave his side, it was still oddly threatening.

Holmes remarked, calmly, "Your right hand would appear to have an unfortunate, reoccurring spasm. My associate is a medical doctor. Perhaps he could examine you and determine the cause. He might be able to offer you some relief from the affliction."

He roared, "I don't need his interference any more than I need yours."

"Pray tell, in what activity are you engaged with which you worry I will interfere?"

Our visitor controlled himself with difficulty. Holmes seemed completely at ease, but I knew that to be mere affectation. Behind his calm, Holmes was ready. I was glad I had my walking stick. "What is it you think you are investigating?" Lord Arbury asked rudely.

"It is no business of yours, but as it is hardly confidential and I have no reason not to disclose it, I will tell you. There have been several pets and farm animals that have disappeared, and I have been hired to investigate it."

He scoffed, "You're here searching for lost sheep? You consider *that* a fit occupation for a 'consulting detective'?"

"I do," affirmed Holmes, "I had already surmised that there is something of import at hand, and your visit has made that conjecture more certain."

"It's that priest, isn't it? He's the one who put you up to this!"

"Priest? Do you mean Rev. Clarke? I am not a religious man, but as I understand it, he is a curate, not a priest."

"Priest? Curate? They are all the same, meddling in people's lives to save their souls, unable to leave folks alone. He goes to London and then you show up. I'll wager that's not coincidence."

"You seem unusually well informed of the curate's travels. Did he try to save your soul? To judge from your manner, it does seem in need of saving."

He roared in anger, so loudly that I was certain he must have been audible to the guests in the common room. This time, he raised his hand, and he pointed it at Holmes. "You meddling, busybody! If you don't leave, you'll regret it."

Holmes remained calm. "I have been threatened by more able men than you. I suggest you need to be the one to leave. Now. If you do not leave voluntarily, I will put you out. I assure you, I am capable of doing so."

Lord Arbury was speechless with anger.

Holmes continued, "I also assure you, it will be as humiliating an experience as I can make it."

His face black with fury, he pushed past us. I could hear the sound of his footsteps as he rushed, more in anger than fear, down the hallway and then the stairs. I could only speculate what the men and women in the main room of the inn would make of his departure with that furious scowl on his face. But Holmes's next words surprised me.

"Watson, come with me."

I followed Holmes to his room. Our rooms had no locks, and Holmes opened the door and stood in its centre. He examined it, moving in a circle. "Someone has been in this room."

"Surely not, Holmes!"

"Most assuredly."

"Mrs. Nithercott, perhaps?"

"Perhaps, but I would like you to examine your belongings, Watson."

I went to my room and entered. To my eyes, it appeared as I had left it, but I opened the drawers of the chest and looked through them. "Everything is here, Holmes."

"Check your medical bag, Watson."

I placed my stick on the bed, knelt down beside it, and brought my medical satchel up from beside the bed. I placed it on the bed beside my stick, sat on the edge, and went quickly through its contents. It was the work of only a few minutes. After a pause to collect my thoughts, I went through it a second time more carefully. No words were required.

"What are you missing, Watson?"

I looked at him, dismayed. "One of my larger surgical scalpels is missing, and two small bottles, one containing laudanum and the other morphine, that I stock for emergencies."

"I will not insult you by asking if you are certain that they were there this morning."

"I am certain they were there when I returned my bag to my room. I have no doubt of it. Holmes, do you think Lord Arbury…?"

Holmes finished my sentence, "Entered our rooms while they were unoccupied and searched through our belongings? Given his personality and the length of time he was here, I recognized it as a possibility. I hadn't realized you had morphine with you, Watson."

"Would that have made a difference?"

"No. I only mention it because I did not know it was part of your regular stock. Morphine can be used as a sedative, can it not?"

I shook my head. "Many laymen believe that to be the case, no doubt, but we in the medical profession use it only to treat severe pain. Once we administer morphine, sleep may indeed come to an individual once the pain is relieved, which may be why some have concluded it is a sedative. Laudanum, another derivative of the poppy, would be more effective in that role. In fact, it is that attribute of laudanum that has made it a popular remedy for many ills, and perhaps one that is over prescribed." Holmes remained unmoving, his chin on his chest. "Holmes, both morphine and laudanum, incorrectly administered, can have harmful consequences, perhaps the least of which is addiction. In overdose, they can be fatal."

"I am aware of that, Watson."

"Should we not do something?"

"What would you suggest? Accuse Lord Arbury of theft? We have no proof, only suspicion. We never saw him in our rooms, and the rooms are without locks. Anyone could have entered them during our absences during the day."

"If we run after him, we can determine if he has them in his pockets."

"I am certain he is well on his way to Arbury Hall in the carriage I noted along the side of the street when our less comfortable transportation arrived. We would be unlikely to procure a conveyance in time to intercept Lord Arbury before he arrived at the hall. Once there, he has only to refuse us admittance. No, Watson, once the possibility occurred to me, I should have insisted that you inventory your belongings to determine if there was anything missing and then insisted on searching him before he left."

I was shocked. "That would have been unpardonably rude."

"I had no intention of begging his pardon."

"What if you had found nothing?"

"I doubt that would have been the result, but we shall never know now."

We were both silent. The enormity of the theft grew in my mind as I considered its ramifications. "Holmes, this is very bad."

"More than you know, Watson."

Before I could respond, there was a timid knock at my door. Holmes raised an eyebrow, and I rose from the bed and opened it. It was Lily Nithercott.

"Good even, Dr. Watson," she said seriously. "Mama says that yer even meal be ready."

I smiled at her. "Please tell your mother that Mr. Holmes and I will be down presently."

"Aye, Dr. Watson. And, please, thank ye for all ye did for Dolly. She be much better."

"As I said this morning, you are most welcome."

She flashed a smile at me. "I be glad ye came."

"I, too."

And she left. I thought to myself what an engaging child she was. Holmes was regarding me with a bemused expression. "Well, at least one resident of Wenlock Edge is content that we are here, or, perhaps, that one of us is here." He looked at me, with respect in his eyes. "You have a way with children, Watson."

I nodded my thanks, but my mind was absorbed by concern that had nothing to do with Lily's short visit. I chose my words with care. "Holmes, why did you say this was worse than I knew."

Holmes's face darkened. "Did you notice Lord Arbury's footwear, Watson?"

The last five years with Holmes had prepared me for unexpected questions like this one, and I responded, "No. I was more concerned with ensuring our safety."

"Yes, I noticed the tight grip you had on your stick. Given the topic of our conversation, it is understandable you did not take notice of his feet. Watson, the toes of his boots were square."

Chapter 8

Holmes's revelation distracted me from my meal and troubled my sleep. The pleasure of our meal, which was superbly moist yet slightly charred venison accompanied by roasted vegetables that were seasoned delicately, only intruded slightly on my thoughts, which grew more and more morbid as I considered our case. Once we retired, I found myself flitting from one alarming thought to the next. Why would a man of Lord Arbury's prominence, a man who, by rights, could sit in the House of Lords, kidnap animals from others' homes and farms? Certainly, he had animals of his own, cared for by hired men on his holdings, and did not need more. And why would he, if indeed it *was* he – because we could not be assured that he and only he wore footwear with squared toes in the village – why would he boil the bones and place them in piles? And with whom was he in league, and why? Why would any human being do these things? Try as I might, I could find no answer to these questions other than insanity.

When we retired for the night, I went to my room and to bed, suspecting that Holmes would remain awake, perhaps smoking his pipe in his room, considering all aspects of the problem that confronted us. If he did not sit in the lone chair furnished with his room, I pictured him pacing the floor, his hands behind his back, his brow lowered and furrowed in concentration. So I had often found him when faced with a difficult conundrum, and this case seemed as impenetrable as any we had encountered.

I woke the next day, surprised to find that I had slept well and was unexpectedly refreshed, for I had never before slept in a rope bed and had thought that it might not agree with me. While perhaps not as comfortable as my own mattress in 221b Baker Street, it had proven surprisingly firm. I had no need to glance at my watch to determine the time. I could estimate that it was early morning by the sunlight already warming my room and by the distant sounds of our hosts moving in the inn. I arose, made my toilet, and was putting on my shoes when I heard Holmes's voice through my door.

"Are you awake, Watson?"

"I am," I responded.

Holmes opened the door and entered. "Perhaps you, like me, thought there could be no further bizarre occurrences in this case outside of the ones we had already discovered or experienced last night, but if so, you were wrong."

"Holmes, whatever do you mean?"

"Gregson is waiting for us. Lord Arbury was murdered last night during his evening meal."

I could not believe my ears. "Gregson? Tobias Gregson? Of Scotland Yard?"

"The same."

"How...Why...?

"Scotland Yard was sent for, no doubt by telegraph, by the local constabulary when Lord Arbury's body was discovered. Scotland Yard engaged a special for Gregson and two constables, and they arrived late last night, or perhaps I should say early this morning. Apparently, when a British lord is murdered, even one who has not sat the House of Lords for nearly a decade, the government takes notice."

"And Lord Arbury was murdered you say?"

"Apparently while still at table, or so I am informed."

"Holmes, this is unbelievable!"

"I would have said incredible, save that I must give it credit."

"I have never encountered anything like this in my life. Surely, nothing else could surprise me now."

"No? Let me make the attempt. You and I are suspects in the murder."

I goggled at him. "Surely not!"

He chuckled. "Well, no longer, but Gregson assures me that until he arrived, we were the main suspects of the local constabulary."

"But why? On what grounds could someone possibly suspect us of murder?"

"Let us join Inspector Gregson and let him tell his story. And take your bag. You may have need of it. And if not, we have learned it is imprudent to leave it behind."

My head nearly spinning from what I had just been told, I took my medical bag and followed Holmes to the main room of the Inn. Gregson, tow-headed, tall, and solid as an oak door, waited for us below, sitting easily in one of the rough, wooden chairs. A young constable, no more than twenty-three, stood by the door. Mrs. Nithercott was behind the bar, silently preparing for the day and watching us intently. Gregson placed one of his heavy, thick hands against the table and pushed himself to his feet.

"Greetings, Doctor Watson. Sleep well?"

"Uncommonly well, thank you, Gregson."

"Not out murdering lords at their suppers during the night?"

"Of course not!"

Roaring with laughter, he fell back into the chair, slamming one hands against the table hard enough that I feared it would collapse. Fortunately, it was stoutly made. After he was done, he wiped his eyes. "This job don't give a man many opportunities for a little fun."

Holmes said drily, "I am gratified that our circumstances could provide you with the odd occasion for amusement."

"Oh, don't be like that, Holmes. Take a joke, man!" He turned to me. "Certainly you can appreciate the irony, Dr. Watson."

"I confess," I responded coldly, "that it escapes me entirely."

Gregson roared again, then rose a second time, mirth still in his voice. Behind him, the constable appeared uncomfortable with Gregson's brand of humour, and he was attempting to conceal that fact. Failing that, he apparently at least hoped to remain unnoticed by his superior. No doubt, it helped that Gregson's back was to him. "You could have knocked me over with a feather when I was told you were here."

"Watson, too, found your presence here equally astonishing. Perhaps you could explain the case against us on the way to Arbury Hall," suggested Holmes. "And we can inform you of our enquiries here. I presume you have one of the Hall carriages waiting."

"Right you are, Holmes." He turned to Mrs. Nithercott. "Thank you for your hospitality, ma'am."

"Ye be most welcome." And she came out from behind the bar and handed Holmes and me each a cloth sack. "Breakfast for ye. It be not much, but it be better than naught."

"Mrs. Nithercott," said Holmes, "not even the most luxurious of London hotels could be so thoughtful." She blushed at Holmes's thanks, and we left with Gregson.

As Holmes had surmised, there was a carriage waiting outside the inn. An older man in green livery waited in the seat, holding the reins. The young constable held the door for us. Holmes and I sat on the bench facing the front, and Gregson sat facing us, his weight so great the carriage sank noticeably upon his entrance. The constable joined Gregson, shutting the door behind him. Gregson knocked on the roof and shouted. "Take us to the hall, my good man!" And the carriage started off. Holmes and I ate our meal, which we learned was a small sandwich of egg and cheese with an appetizing sauce.

Between bites, Holmes said, "I hope you didn't hurt yourself when you fell, Gregson."

"Nah. It was just a... I said nothing about a fall!"

Holmes pointed. "There is a slight stain of dirt on your right pants leg." Gregson involuntarily glanced at it. "And an even fainter, but equally visible mark on the ball of your right hand. There was an attempt to remove the dirt from both, but it was only partially successful, no doubt because the dirt was ground deeply into the cloth and your hand, indicating either that you had intentionally pressed dirt into your pants with your right hand or you fell heavily, using your right hand to break your fall. I considered the first unlikely."

Gregson, who was as familiar as I was with Holmes's observational powers, possibly more so for he had known Holmes longer, grunted. "I had a misstep at the Hall this morning. And the only thing hurt was my dignity."

"I am pleased to learn you suffered no injury." Holmes turned to the constable. "And I regret you were pulled away from your family with so little notice."

Wide-eyed, the young constable looked at Gregson, who said, "Don't ask, Fiddick. It only encourages him."

The corner of Holmes's mouth turned up in a ghost of a smile, and I decided to intervene. "Are we really accused of murdering Lord Arbury?"

Gregson said, "Not if I have anything to say about it, and I do. It was that ass, the sheriff here." He searched for the name. "Headman? Header?"

Constable Fiddick spoke. "Hender, sir. Otis Hender."

"Thank you. Hender. He's an ass. The first thing he did was accuse you and Mr. Holmes of the crime."

"And his grounds?"

"You were heard to have a fight with His Lordship last night."

Holmes smiled thinly. "Well, I did offer to put him out by force if he did not leave voluntarily."

Gregson eyed Holmes keenly. "Did you now?"

"Yes. He had the temerity to threaten me if I did not complete my investigation forthwith and leave on the next train back to London." There was a pause. "I did not take kindly to the invitation."

"No one would. Rather high-handed that. So, what is this investigation of yours? Does it have a bearing on His Lordship's murder?"

"I can only presume it has," Holmes responded, and then he proceeded to explain the disappearance of animals that had brought us to Wenlock Edge, including our grisly discovery at the abbey.

When he was done, Gregson said, "You get the oddest cases, Holmes. Well, you can leave your animals for another day. You have the murder of a member of the House of Lords to investigate. I don't see how missing animals can be related to a murder, do you?"

Holmes said, "Not at present, but then, I have only just learned of the murder. I am not nearly as confident as you that the two cases are unrelated. I presume you are certain it was murder?"

Gregson grunted. "His Lordship has a knife sticking out of his back. I would say that makes the theory inarguable."

"Indeed. The way you phrased your sentence would lead the listener to conclude the knife is still there. Is it?"

"Yes. When I learned you were here and cleared up the fact that you couldn't possibly have had a motive – much less an opportunity – to do His Lordship in, I thought I would request your help. We'll pay you the usual rates. Don't think my superiors will balk at it, seeing it's a lord and all. It's a puzzling enough case. Know you like those. Knowing how you work, I decided to leave everything as it was, completely undisturbed."

"I am most gratified, Gregson."

I asked, "How did you determine our innocence?"

Gregson replied, "I presumed it, but I thought my superiors would be unimpressed with my faith in you without some corroboration. I talked to some who were at the inn last night. Apparently, while His Lordship could be heard roaring like a dock hand who had stubbed his toe and left with a face black with anger, no one heard your voice or that of Mr. Holmes. The innkeeper and his wife, as well as some others, verified that you ate at the inn after the incident, and remembered you were in plain sight when we believe the murder was committed." He shook his head. "And even then, that ass insisted you must have gone to your rooms, climbed out your windows, and somehow made it there and back all without anyone the wiser."

"At what time was the murder committed?"

"The butler served his dinner at eight o'clock. The body was discovered shortly before nine."

"His Lordship ate alone?"

"Last night, he did. His wife, sons, and daughter-in-law had eaten earlier."

"Odd, that."

"There's a lot about this murder that is odd. When you get there, you'll see what I mean. Not a lot of tears being shed in the house. But there's one thing worse than all the others. It's made this a devil of a case to solve, and it's why I'm calling you in."

"Oh?" asked Holmes. "You have my attention, Gregson."

"The wife, both sons, and the daughter-in-law have all confessed to the murder, and each one says he acted alone."

Chapter 9

We arrived at Arbury Hall shortly after Gregson's astonishing statement. This close, the Hall was an imposing, three-storey structure of grey stone, with a large, main hall and two wings on each side. Each window was ringed with stone that seemed to angle away from the frames. Black shutters were on the sides of each window. There were two balconies facing the road, one on each wing. The roofline was dotted with stone chimneys. Despite the fact that there were no visible signs of neglect, it somehow projected the appearance of wear.

We alighted from the carriage and entered Arbury Hall. The entryway was a magnificent, oval room with matching staircases curving on each side. The room was ablaze with light. Another constable, a brawny young man who was actually larger than Gregson, stood at attention at the doorway.

Gregson acknowledged him. "Penhale"

"Inspector."

"Anything new?"

"Lady Arbury asked if she could send for the Vicar to provide spiritual comfort."

"And?"

The constable looked uncomfortable. "I saw no harm in it, sir."

"Neither do I."

Constable Penhale looked considerably relieved. "He's up with her now, sir."

Holmes asked innocently, "Were the biscuits that accompanied the tea fresh, Constable?"

Gregson threw a piercing glance at Holmes. Penhale opened his mouth in astonishment, but he managed to respond, "Very fresh, sir. Some of the best biscuits I ever had."

Gregson eyed him. "You had tea?" It was more an accusation than a question.

"Yes, sir."

"I believe I told you not to leave this post."

Holmes intervened. "The constable did not leave his post, Gregson. The tea was brought to him."

Gregson turned on Holmes. "How the devil do you know all this?" he demanded.

Holmes murmured, "Crumbs, inspector." He pointed to the front of the constable's uniform and the floor. "No doubt, the tray was placed on that convenient table beside the door."

Penhale looked at Holmes as if he was a supernatural being. More familiar with Holmes's powers of deduction, Gregson was less impressed. He repeated to the constable, "So, you had tea."

"Yes, sir."

"Didn't see any harm in that, either, I suppose?"

"No, sir." By strength of will, Penhale managed not to shift back and forth on his feet like an errant schoolboy. "We had been up all night sir, and I hadn't had my breakfast."

As I well knew from some of Holmes's past cases in which I participated, Gregson could be a hard man, but in this instance, he relented. "I could do with a spot of tea myself," he said. "As you've had yours already, see if you can scrounge up some for Constable Fiddick and me."

Penhale nodded in the direction of Holmes and me. "And your guests, sir?"

"I just watched them eat their ruddy breakfasts in the carriage, but if they want more, they can have some, I'm sure." And then he muttered, "It's not like Arbury is going to be needing his."

"I have no need of tea," said Holmes. "Watson?"

"I have eaten my fill."

Gregson nodded and instructed Fiddick to stay at the door, motioning for Holmes and me to follow. "I don't know why I bother with the door. This place has enough ways to the outside I'd need an army of constables to secure it."

"A matter of form, perhaps?" suggested Holmes.

"Just so. And discipline. Do you want to talk with the family first, or see the body?"

"The body," said Holmes without hesitation. "I would not want to delay your itinerary. No doubt, you will want to remove it as soon as I'm done."

"That I will."

"Has the medical examiner examined the body?"

Gregson shook his head in the negative. "Ours didn't accompany us, though he should be on his way. This backwater doesn't have one." He looked at me. "I see you have your bag, Doctor."

I responded to the implication. "I am not a pathologist, Inspector."

"Well, do your best to give us an idea until the London medical examiner arrives, not that there's any doubt as to the cause of death. Pretty obvious, that knife."

He stopped in front of doors I assumed led to the dining room. "It's in here. Do you want me along?"

Holmes said, "There's no need, Gregson, unless you want to watch. Go, break your fast."

"Then I'll leave you to it." And he matched deed with word and quitted us.

Holmes opened the door, and we entered the dining room.

It was nearly as large as the entryway. Dark, walnut panelling lined each wall from the floor to a height of about five feet. Above the panelling was plaster, painted an off white, that soared at least another ten feet until it met the tray ceiling from which hung a massive golden chandelier. In the middle of the room, directly under the chandelier, was a long table that could easily have seated thirty. Five high-backed chairs that stood nearly as tall as a man were grouped at the centre of the table, some on each side, while additional identical chairs lined the walls between serving boards and tables. At the middle of the dining table, on the other side and difficult to see because of the chairs facing him, was the body of a man. He had fallen over the remains of his meal. Had he been sitting erect, he would have been facing us. At the right was a large fireplace, now without a fire. The table and chairs rested not on the wooden floor, but on a large, thick Persian carpet in blue, gold, and red designs against a beige background.

Beside me, Holmes tensed in anger. I glanced at him.

"It is well Gregson left the scene undisturbed, or I doubt I would be able to discover anything amid the trampling. If I didn't know better, I would conclude half of Scotland Yard had been through this room in the last twelve hours."

I said nothing, and Holmes looked at me. Slowly, his anger evaporated. "Well, it can't be helped now, and no doubt Gregson meant well. Watson, why don't you see to His Lordship?"

I started around to the side of the table farthest from us on which the body lay. Holmes approached the table on the near side, examining everything, and I could see by the glint in his eyes that something interested him keenly. As I approached the body of Lord Arbury, Holmes turned from the table, withdrew his magnifying glass from his inverness, and began examining the rug.

Lord Arbury, for it was the same man who had accosted us at The Good Lady, had collapsed over his plate almost as if he had decided to nap in his food, except that his face was convulsed in rictus. He had froth around his mouth, a mute witness to his mortal agony. Uneaten food was pressed against his cheek. He was dressed as we had seen him the previous night. A large kitchen knife was embedded in his back. Surprisingly, given the obvious cause of death, there was no tell-tale red or pink discernible in the froth around his mouth. I had expected that, as a knife wound that penetrates that heart or lungs often results in traces of blood in the mouth as haemorrhaging brings death. Dessert plates, four in all, were still on the table with silverware and tall, fluted glasses for wine, though I noticed two strange things. One dessert plate had no wine glass, and the glass in front of His Lordship had four dark smudges under the brim, three smudges on one side and one on the other.

But as odd as this was, I had no time to fathom why these things might be so, for a far more jarring discovery commanded my entire concentration. "Holmes, there is no blood."

Holmes, still on his hands and knees and now examining the carpet beside the fireplace and wall, responded, "I made note of that Watson. What do you deduce from it?"

"He could not possibly have been killed here."

"Nor could he have been killed in those clothes, at least by knife," Holmes added. He then made a pleased sound of discovery. Again reaching into his inverness, he withdrew a small chemist's envelope and tweezers. I watched as he inserted the tweezers into the thick pile of the carpet, extracted what appeared to be a shard of glass, and transferred it into the envelope. He did this three more times before he appeared satisfied and folded the envelope shut. "I should have looked here first. It should have been obvious from the start that they would be here rather than closer to the table." His remark led me to assume he had expected to find shards of glass, though I had no idea what had led him to that conclusion.

Then he went to the fireplace. "In all likelihood, I am wasting my time, Watson, but we can hope our killer neglected to burn everything. Ah! We're in luck!" Again using his tweezers, he pulled out a scrap of paper from the ashes. "This is more than I could have hoped for, Watson! Look at this."

I approached him as he held the scrap of paper out to me, barely a sliver, and I could see it was the upper left corner of a postal envelope. The numbers "4367" and the letter "A" followed by what possibly might have been a "c", though because of the charring it could really have been anything. The rest of the envelope had been burned, and the edges of the fragment were black.

"Holmes, how did you know to look for this?"

"Did you not notice the smudges on His Lordship's wine glass, Watson?"

"I did, but I made nothing of it."

"It was obvious to me they had been left by fingers that had already become stained with ash."

"But there were only four smudges, Holmes, not five."

"Ah, Watson, think! If you pick up a wine glass from the top, and not the bottom, the first three fingers of the hand grip one side of the brim, and the thumb the opposing side. The little finger is too short to touch the glass. If your fingers had already been blackened by soot because you tossed an envelope into the fire, you would leave four smudges, not five."

While confident Holmes was correct, I was still puzzled. "But Holmes, why pick up the glass at all?"

"Because it wasn't His Lordship's glass," answered Holmes. "I surmise that Lord Arbury threw his glass in anger at his murderer, missed him, and the glass shattered here against the fireplace."

"The glass shards you picked up!"

"Yes, Watson. Once I saw the smudges and noticed a wine glass was missing, I went hunting first for indications of broken glass, and second for anything that might indicate what had been burned."

"But where are the rest of the pieces from the shattered glass?"

"Gone, Watson. These small shards were overlooked. Now, what did you discover about the cause of death?"

I was confused by the question. "As I said, Holmes, there is insufficient blood. Lord Arbury could not have been killed here."

"I beg to differ, Watson. To repeat myself, he could not have been killed here *by knife*."

"But, Holmes, he has a knife in his back."

Holmes chuckled. "Watson, you are a good man and an even better physician, but you lack imagination. You already noticed there is insufficient blood in this room to account for death by knife, but there is also insufficient blood on His Lordship's clothing to account for him being stabbed somewhere else and then carried here. And I point out, these are the same clothes he was wearing when we last saw him."

I was bewildered. "Could he have been murdered while wearing other clothing? Isn't it customary for those in his position to change before dinner?"

Holmes nodded. "Of course you are correct, Watson. That is the custom of many who have servants. But consider the scene. Arbury arrives from The Good Lady, seething from his encounter with us, and changes for dinner. He eats part of his meal, but then, for some reason, he leaves the table with his meal partially eaten. Unnoticed by anyone, he leaves the dining room and has an unfortunate encounter with his murderer, who stabs him in ambush from behind. The murderer then withdraws the knife, removes His Lordship's dinner clothing, dresses him in the attire he wore at the inn, carries or drags the corpse back to the dining room – also unobserved – places him back at table, and thoughtfully reinserts the knife so as to leave us no doubt about the cause of death. It's preposterous."

"When you put it like that, Holmes, it is unbelievable."

"And so," my friend replied, "I do not believe it. I search for another explanation."

At that point, Gregson entered the room. "Well, Mr. Holmes, did you find anything?"

Holmes opened the chemist's envelope and showed him the glass shards. "These were beside the fireplace. Did you remove pieces of broken glass before our arrival?"

"No, we did not."

"I thought as much. And yet, I found these shards of glass here," said Holmes, pointing to the spot he had found them. "Someone removed pieces of broken glass last night, Gregson, before your arrival."

"How in heaven's name do you know the glass wasn't broken days ago?"

"Because," said Holmes patiently, "there are only four wine glasses at table, and there should be five. I surmised that the missing wine class had been shattered, thrown perhaps, and investigation proved that surmise to be correct. But no matter," he continued. "I found the shards beside the fireplace and I found this among the ashes inside it." He showed the burnt fragment to Gregson.

"Shame the entire return address isn't visible. You might have had something."

Holmes said nothing, but his silence spoke as loudly to Gregson as any words might have done.

Gregson answered the unspoken criticism. "You believe this is important?"

"Almost certainly," replied Holmes.

"How?"

"I cannot say at this time, but I hope to be able to do so within twenty-four hours. Did you remark the lack of blood?"

"I did. Strange, that."

"Impossible, I would have said."

Gregson grunted. "So, what is your theory?"

"That he was poisoned while at his meal. If your chemist analyses these shards, he may find traces of it. If not there, then in the food."

"What kind of poison should he look for?"

Holmes raised his eyebrows. "I'm not a magician, Gregson, to know without chemical analysis, but if I were a betting man, I would put my money on strychnine. It is readily available and quick acting, but not so rapid in its effect that a man would be unable to react before succumbing to it." And then he added, "A man who consumed strychnine would be almost certain to know it within five minutes of ingestion. Frothing at the mouth is a common reaction to strychnine poisoning."

I knew that Holmes was an expert in poisons, and I had little doubt he would be proven correct, having noticed the froth around Lord Arbury's mouth myself.

Gregson asked, "Then why the knife?"

"The logical conclusion would be to prevent us from, or at least delay us in, knowing the actual cause of His Lordship's demise because the cause of death itself would identify – or at least strongly indicate – the murderer."

We were silent while the three of us considered Holmes's words. Finally, Holmes broke the silence. "It would be good to speak to the family now, individually if possible."

But before Gregson could respond, another man burst into the room, followed by Constable Penhale who said, "I beg your pardon, sir, but I could not stop him."

The man who had preceded Penhale was of normal height, but appeared shorter in relation his girth, which was considerable. Dressed in a brown jacket, green tweed pants, and a dull orange vest that was straining at the buttons, he presented an odd appearance, as if he had selected his attire completely at random. A large badge of some kind was pinned to his lapel. His face was pale, which made the thinning of his dusty brown hair even more noticeable.

He wasted no time in making his displeasure known. "What be ye doing bringing these men here? They be wanted for questioning in the murder of Lord Arbury! Be Scotland Yard this incompetent?"

In my experience, Gregson was never one to contain his temper, but he managed to do so now. Had I been this man, I would have been wary, but the intruder was too angry to give Gregson's uncharacteristic reticence a thought. And, of course, he didn't know Gregson as well as I did. "Ah, Headman," said Gregson. "I'm glad you're here."

"Hender!" snapped the man. "Sherriff Otis Hender. Can't ye even be getting me name correct?"

Blandly, Gregson replied, "Thank you, *Hender*. I will want to get your name correct when I make my report."

"Ye have brought these men...."

Gregson interrupted him. "Sheriff Hender, please permit me to introduce to you Sherlock Holmes and Dr. John Watson, men known to Scotland Yard, both of whom who have provided service to the Her Majesty's police on several occasions."

Hender was taken aback and gaped unappealingly in response. Gregson continued with no little amount of smugness in his voice. "I have already thoroughly investigated your claims that these men left the inn and murdered Lord Arbury. I assure you, both were in full view of some twenty patrons as well as the owners of your local inn while eating their evening meals. It is beyond question that when Lord Arbury was murdered, they were nowhere near Arbury Hall. That is how *incompetent* Scotland Yard is, Mr. Hender. In less than twelve hours we have completely exonerated your main suspects." And then, after a pause, he added, "You can be sure that fact, and your name, will feature prominently in my report."

Hender's face turned white with rage. "Ye be daft. They argued with His Lordship when they be told to leave."

Gregson remained impassive, which, given the provocation, was no mean feat. "In doing so, they have broken no laws, Hender. No man, not even a member of the House of Lords, can demand that a man leave a public place against his will."

"They be troublemakers!"

Holmes broke into the conversation, his voice mild. "Sheriff Hender, how did you know Lord Arbury demanded that we leave Wenlock Edge?"

He sputtered. "Why, it be known!"

"How? It was the subject of a private conversation. Outside of Inspector Gregson and Constable Fiddick, Watson and I have spoken to no one about the substance of that conversation. How is it that you know what Lord Arbury instructed us to do?"

Hender blinked in surprise, then responded to Holmes, his voice less truculent. "It be known. Lord Arbury be shouting it out."

"Not that portion of the conversation," returned Holmes evenly. "And I doubt the import of his words, even shouted, would have carried to the common room of the inn in such a manner that what he said could be understood."

"It be known!" the sheriff repeated, raising his voice in what I thought was an attempt to hide his own uncertainty.

Gregson finally lost his temper. "Alright! That's enough! Hender, this investigation is in the hands of Scotland Yard. I will inform you if your services are needed in the future."

Sheriff Hender scowled at Gregson. "Ye'll be needing me help. I know the area and people, and ye do not."

"I will let you know when you may be of assistance. For right now, your services are no longer required." When Hender began to object, Gregson turned to Fiddick. "Constable, please escort Sheriff Hender outside. Make sure he doesn't get lost on the way."

"Yes, sir."

Still objecting, Hender was taken by the arm and firmly escorted from the room.

Gregson said, "He's an ass."

Holmes said, "That may be, but he is an inexplicably well-informed ass." After a pause, he added, "Inspector, you asked me earlier if I thought the reason Watson and I are here was related to the death of Lord Arbury."

"That I did, and told you I don't see how they are."

"Nor do I, and yet now that I have made the acquaintance of the truculent Sheriff Hender, I grow more certain that the two cases are intertwined."

Gregson closed his eyes as if weary, and he brought a hand to his forehead. "Does that really matter?" he asked, and I was reminded that he and his constables had been awake all night. When Gregson lowered his hand, he was once again alert. "You said you wanted to speak with the family."

"Indeed."

Gregson said grimly, "We'll see if it's possible."

Chapter 10

It turned out not to be possible. The first hurdle that faced us was the physical collapse of Lady Arbury. Gregson rang for the butler and requested that Lady Arbury meet us in the sitting room, which had been set aside for use by Scotland Yard. The butler, Travers, was tall, dignified, somewhat stout, immaculately dressed, and proper. When he returned, he said, "I regret to inform you that Lady Arbury is indisposed at the moment. I have sent for her physician, but I have been informed he is attending a childbirth and may be delayed. She is being cared for by her sons, daughter-in-law, and the local curate."

"Indisposed, you say?"

"Yes, sir. Recent events have left her greatly distraught."

"She seemed fine earlier this morning," said Gregson, with a tone that I had seen unnerve more than one constable.

Travers was unimpressed by Gregson's intimidating tone and replied calmly, "Indeed, so she was, sir. Earlier. But then she learned that Master Bradford and Master Patrick had both confessed to murdering their father. It affected her deeply."

"No doubt it was quite a shock," returned Gregson unkindly, "since she had already told me that she had murdered her husband herself, alone and unaided."

Travers remained silent.

"What did she think of her daughter-in-law confessing to the same murder?"

"I couldn't say, sir. I don't believe she knows."

Holmes said, "Mr. Travers, who served Lord Arbury his evening meal?"

"I did, sir."

"Alone?"

"Yes, sir. The rest of the family had already dined and were beginning dessert. Lord Arbury had just returned from the village. I dismissed the remaining staff."

"Why? Were they not necessary to serve dessert?"

Travers managed not to look uncomfortable, but the short pause before he answered Holmes was telling. "Normally, yes, I would have retained the staff to serve dessert."

"Why didn't you?"

He cleared his throat. "His Lordship was unusually…wroth. Seeing his ill humour, Her Ladyship and the family retired soon after his arrival. I was quite capable of serving His Lordship alone. The additional staff was no longer necessary, and I dismissed them."

Having experienced only a small sample of Lord Arbury's anger, I wondered if, perhaps, Travers had been attempting to shield the rest of the servants from his employer's temper, which was no doubt well known in the household. I could not prevent myself from feeling that it was rather decent of him.

"When was this?"

"Shortly after eight o'clock."

"How did Lord Arbury account for his anger?"

"He did not account for it at all, sir."

"So, you served his meal?"

"I did."

"Did he eat and drink the same food as the rest of the family?"

"Yes, sir."

"Served from the same dishes on the sideboard?"

"Yes, sir."

"And the same bottle of wine?"

"Yes, sir, though Her Ladyship prefers sherry and had that with her meal."

"But the others had the same wine?"

"Yes, sir."

"Did you stay in attendance on His Lordship during his meal?"

"I did not, sir."

"Why not?"

"He dismissed me."

"Why?"

"I could not say, sir. It was not for me to ask."

"Did anyone else enter the room or talk with Lord Arbury after your dismissal?"

Travers paused noticeably before answering, "I couldn't say, sir."

Despite the fact that Travers's face hadn't noticeably altered, I was nearly certain he was lying. To my surprise, Holmes did not pursue his line of questioning. Instead, he said, "Who collected the broken fragments of the wineglass beside the fireplace and where were they disposed?"

Travers raised his eyebrows. "Broken fragments of a wine glass? I am sure you are mistaken, sir. No wine glass was broken."

"None? Never?"

"Not to my knowledge, sir."

Holmes let the air vibrate with the butler's words before turning to Gregson. "Perhaps it would be best if we modified my original intention." He turned to Travers. "You have told us Her Ladyship has had a great shock, and I understand that she and her entire family have confessed to the murder of His Lordship. Inspector Gregson is of Scotland Yard, and he cannot ignore those confessions. We can wait for her physician to arrive, but that will only delay the inevitable. We must talk with her. It is unavoidable."

Before Travers could answer, another voice intervened. "I can help with that."

A young man of perhaps thirty years of age stood at the open door. He was handsome and broad shouldered, and I could see a resemblance to the murdered lord, though on him, the features were kinder. I assumed that this would of necessity be one of his sons, an assumption that was confirmed when he introduced himself. "I am Bradford Arbury, eldest son of Lord Arbury. You have no need to question Mother. I killed my father. She had nothing to do with it."

Gregson snorted.

Distraught, Travers said, "Master Bradford!"

"It's alright, Travers. You can go. I'll handle this."

A flicker of concern crossed Travers's face, and he said, "As you wish, Master Bradford, but I must first state in the presence of these men that, to my knowledge, you left the dining Hall with Lady Arbury, your wife, and Master Patrick and did not return to the Hall at any time."

Bradford smiled. "Loyal to the end, Travers. You're a good man. But I must confess to my crimes. You may be excused."

"Very good, sir." But to judge from his expression, Travers did not appear to believe it to be good. He was deeply troubled, and he left with anxiety written on his face.

When he was gone, Bradford Arbury said, "I killed my father. Don't listen to Travers. He is an old family servant. He would give his right arm to protect any of us from harm, and he would certainly not balk at lying. After we left the old man alone, I returned."

"Indeed?" responded Holmes. "Why did you return?"

"My reasons are unimportant."

Holmes said, "Perhaps. Perhaps not. How did you kill him?"

A look of disgust appeared on the young man's face. "Isn't it obvious? I shoved a knife in his back while he was eating."

Holmes responded. "Convince me."

Bradford Arbury was startled. "What do you mean?"

"Convince me it was you and not your mother, your brother, or your wife." He continued with an arched eyebrow, "My understanding is that you have all confessed to the crime."

"My mother, wife, and brother are lying. They are trying to protect me."

"And how do I and Inspector Gregson know *you* aren't lying to protect *them*?"

He seemed offended. "I give you my word."

Gregson exploded, "Well, hens in a handbasket, that solves it all! You give your word! As if you all haven't given me your ruddy word! I have half a mind to run the lot of you in and present you to the prosecuting barrister as a group!" He turned to my friend. "You see how it is, Holmes?"

"I do indeed, Inspector. Would you permit me to continue questioning Mr. Arbury?"

"With my blessing. And you can go after the rest of the family, too. I wish you luck getting more out of them than I have."

Holmes returned to Bradford Arbury, his eyes piercing. "Do you still intend not to reveal your reasons for murdering your father?"

Bradford looked uncomfortable. "I would rather not say."

Gregson informed Holmes, "It is as if they are reading from the same hymnal. None of them would rather say."

Holmes was unruffled. "It will be difficult to obtain a conviction for murder, even with a confession, absent of a credible motive for committing it. Where did you get the knife, Mr. Arbury?"

If the situation were not so serious, the look of surprise on Bradford Arbury's face would have been comical. To my eyes, it appeared that he had not considered the need to account for acquiring the murder weapon, and he was now searching for an explanation to do so. He finally arrived at a solution.

"It was there."

"Indeed. Where is 'there,' Mr. Arbury?"

"Beside him."

"Your father, you mean."

"Yes. Just so." He seemed relieved and spoke with more confidence. "The knife was beside my father. I picked it up and shoved it in his back."

"But this was a large, kitchen knife, Mr. Arbury. It might be on the sideboard for cutting meat, but hardly at table with His Lordship."

Bradford began to perspire. "I misspoke. I did not mean the knife was beside my father at table. It was on the sideboard, near my father."

"Mr. Bradford, if you cannot lie better than this, you are wasting the time of everyone here. I would appreciate it if you made more of an effort to deceive me. You are making this too easy. I made note that there was a carving knife at the sideboard. You did not pick up the knife from the sideboard."

"There were two knives there. I picked up the largest."

Drily, Holmes said, "Interesting. That is an unusual serving arrangement. Shall we call for Mr. Travers and ask him to corroborate your statement, Mr. Arbury? Or the kitchen staff?"

Bradford pressed his lips together, then finally answered, "I told you, you shouldn't listen to Travers. The rest of the serving staff is equally loyal and should not be believed."

Gregson made an inarticulate and involuntary sound of anger, and then contained himself with an effort. We knew Bradford Arbury was lying. Holmes's conclusion from the evidence that that Lord Arbury had been poisoned, while not confirmed as yet, seemed unassailable. I could only speculate as to why Holmes was withholding our conclusion from Lord Arbury's oldest son.

Ignoring Gregson's obvious frustration, Bradford Arbury reaffirmed, "I assure you, I am telling you the truth."

Holmes held up a hand, palm outward. "Please, Mr. Arbury, refrain from insulting our intelligence any further. You had no more to do with murdering your father by knife than Inspector Gregson here, and the sooner you and your family cooperate with us, the sooner we will resolve this mystery."

We stood silently after his remark, Bradford Arbury in wounded dignity, Gregson in badly controlled anger, and Holmes in a heightened state of readiness. Finally, Holmes said, "Mr. Arbury, you can see how it is. Mr. Gregson is reaching the end of his patience, and I cannot say I find fault with him for that. Did you overhear the topic of our conversation when you arrived earlier?"

"I did."

"Then you know we must speak with your mother and the rest of your family."

"I cannot permit that. My mother is ill. The others are caring for her."

"I assure you, sir, you have no choice. You cannot prevent us from speaking with your family. Your mother may delay the inevitable, but she must speak with Scotland Yard. It is inescapable. Permit me to propose a compromise."

Arbury appeared distrustful. "A compromise?"

"Yes. Watson here is a London physician of no small reputation." I thought that to be a stretch of the truth, but I said nothing, anticipating what my friend planned to suggest. Holmes was continuing. "I propose you let him attend your mother. If he believes your mother too ill to speak with us, we will wait until he believes her stronger or your local physician gives us permission." Holmes turned to me. "I presume you would be willing, Watson."

"Assuredly," I affirmed.

Arbury turned his look of distrust, now almost alarm, to me. He returned to Holmes. "He could say anything."

I interrupted. "I assure you, Mr. Arbury, that I would not betray my medical oaths, not even for Scotland Yard or my closest friend. They are sacrosanct."

Before Arbury could speak, Holmes added, "Moreover, I will agree to interviewing your mother in the presence of the entire family. You and your brother can witness the exchange. Indeed, it might prove helpful to my enquiries. I will even allow your local vicar to remain, if you so wish. It may fortify your mother to have her family and spiritual counsellor in the room. If so, I have no objection to them remaining."

Gregson betrayed a small measure of surprise, and Holmes added, "I assume, Gregson, that you spoke with the family and staff individually earlier."

"That I did," the inspector confirmed.

"Then I no longer see a need to speak with each member separately now." Holmes looked at Arbury. "Well, sir?"

"I... this is very good of you. I would like time to present your offer to the members of my family prior to accepting."

"Please, do so."

After a moment of hesitation, he nodded and left the room. Gregson lost no time in addressing Holmes. "Taking them all together? Are you sure that's wise? Better to take them one at a time, don't you think, and compare their stories after?"

"You have already spoken to them individually, and they have been together since then. If collusion is their aim, they have had sufficient time to alter their stories and ensure they agree if they had not already done so before you arrived from London. No, we will learn nothing from them individually. But collectively, when I reveal to them that I believe His Lordship was poisoned and not dispatched with a kitchen knife? Ah! It might be most revealing to see how they attempt to alter their story, to whom they look for leadership, and at whom they glance fearfully."

"So, that's your game. Wondered why you didn't say anything about poison."

I entered the conversation. "If I may?"

"Always, Watson."

"Why not do what Gregson suggested and charge them all with the crime?"

Holmes answered, "I doubt the inspector spoke in earnest."

Gregson shook his head. "Mr. Holmes is quite right. If I arrested the lot of them, all of them claiming they acted alone, the Crown could not possibly take it to trial. The defence would merely put each member of the family on the stand to exonerate the other." And then he added, "Though I'll wager the judge wouldn't take kindly to it."

"Even worse, from my point of view," said Holmes, "is that we might never know who actually committed the murder or the motives behind it. Who are they protecting? Could it be that each member of the family is convinced, incorrectly, that another family member has committed the murder when, in truth, none of them committed it? Or has one of them, the actual murderer, manipulated the remaining members of the family to obtain their cooperation in providing false confessions? No, Watson, we must know more than this, and Gregson must have proof other than conflicting confessions before presenting a case to the Crown for prosecution."

"I see the difficulty," I replied, at almost the same time that Bradford Arbury returned.

He seemed in full control of himself, and after gaining our attention, he said, "My mother and family accept your offer."

Chapter 11

Holmes and Gregson remained in the sitting room while Bradford Arbury led me up the left staircase in the main entryway to the first floor, and then down the hallway. After passing several doors, he stopped and knocked on one, then entered saying, "It's me, Mother." I followed after him, and he said, "Mother, this is Doctor Watson. Doctor Watson, may I present to you my mother, Lady Arbury."

Lady Arbury was resting in her bed, propped by pillows into a partially sitting position. She was very pale, but her oval face had the promise that, had the situation been different, she would have been a handsome woman. Her hair was iron grey, undone, and fell limply on either side of her face. Even reclined, she exuded a kind of dignity and assurance.

"I am sorry to intrude on your grief and regret making your acquaintance under these circumstances."

"That is most gracious of you, Dr. Watson."

Bradford Arbury continued introductions. "My brother, Patrick, and my wife, Marion. And I believe you have already met Rev. Clarke."

We exchanged strained greetings. Patrick Arbury resembled his father and brother, though his hair was a lighter shade of brown and his shoulders less broad. In addition, while his father's face was powerful in arrogance and his brother's carriage one of strength, there was weakness in the look of Patrick Arbury. He barely met my eyes when he acknowledged me, and he returned to looking at the floor after he had done so. Marion Arbury was sitting in a chair in front of her brother-in-law. Her hair was nearly impossibly black, and her skin bronzed. The contrast with her mother-in-law was striking.

Rev. Clarke was sitting on the edge of another chair on the opposite side of the bed. "Dr. Watson," he said, "I hope you can help us."

"I shall do my utmost." I looked at Lady Arbury. "May I?"

"By all means," she assented.

I sat on the side of the bed and removed my stethoscope from my bag, happy at Holmes's foresight that ensured I had it with me. Lady Arbury submitted to my examination quietly. I listened to her heart and took her pulse. Now closer to her, I could see that she was pale not only from nature, but from the judicial use of cosmetics. Her eyes were circled by weariness, and her cheeks sunken. The others watched in silence as I completed my examination. When I finished, Lady Arbury looked at me with a ghost of a smile on her face.

"Well, Doctor, will I live?"

I returned her smile. "Most assuredly. Your heart and pulse are strong. To my eyes, your colour is pale, but only your regular physician would know for certain if that were out of the ordinary." And then I grew serious. "But then, I'm certain that you knew all this, Lady Arbury."

Bradford Arbury said, "Doctor Watson!"

His mother stopped him with a motion. "Bradford, the doctor is quite right. I have felt better for hours, and I am certain that I could have made it to the sitting room if I only had a reason for doing so. I have been prolonging my convalescence shamelessly, hoping for more time to talk you and Patrick out of this ridiculous and futile gesture on my behalf." She looked at me. "I murdered my husband, Doctor Watson, and wish to pay for my crimes, but my children insist on taking the blame themselves."

Patrick Arbury spoke for the first time, "Mother, you know that isn't true. I killed Papa."

Still looking at me, Lady Arbury said, "Patrick couldn't possibly have murdered his father. I remember when he brought me a baby starling that had fallen out if its nest. He doesn't have the heart for violence."

I ventured to ask, "But you do?"

"I must have, since I committed a violent murder." When I hesitated, she added, "Do you not believe me, Doctor Watson?"

Rev. Clarke spoke for the first time. "None of us believe you, Lady Arbury."

"You wound me, Rev. Clarke. Which of my sons do you believe over me, then?"

"I am not certain I believe any of you, my lady."

Marion Arbury said, "Mama-in-law, I think you must drop this pretence, along with my dear husband and Patrick. I was the one who killed Papa-in-law."

Lady Arbury gave her a sharp look, glanced at her sons and saw immediately that they had known of this fourth confession which I could see took her by surprise. She shot a look of controlled censure at her daughter-in-law. "That is unnecessary and most foolish, my dear."

She almost shrank from the look Lady Arbury gave her, but then rallied and stood her ground. "Not nearly so foolish as what you are doing, Mama-in-law."

Distraught at witnessing such a private exchange, I intervened. "I am not the man you must convince, Lady Arbury."

"I know. I must convince that policeman."

"Even more so than Scotland Yard, you must convince Sherlock Holmes."

"Yes. The detective. Rev. Clarke has been speaking of him. Is he really as astute as he relates? Certainly, those stories in *The Strand* are exaggerated."

"My lady, I myself wrote those stories, quite against Mr. Holmes's will, to ensure he received due credit for his work. Far from exaggerations, they are completely accurate. I have been honoured to have known Sherlock Holmes these five years, and in that time, I have seen him unravel mysteries that would certainly have gone without solution except for his intervention. In my experience, he is without equal, and worthy of your trust."

She looked at me speculatively. "That is high praise."

"It is the certain truth, Lady Arbury," I responded without hesitation. "I will not retract a word I have said."

She looked at her eldest son, then to the curate. After a moment, she said to her daughter-in-law, "Marion, have Travers bring Mr. Holmes up with the inspector. We must have this out."

"Mama-in-law, you should rest."

"There is no rest for the wicked, my dear, and I have been very wicked. I broke a commandment, after all: thou shalt not kill. Now, please do as I have asked."

Averting her face to prevent us from seeing her tears, Marion Arbury, left the room. As we waited, I returned my medical tools to my bag. Several times, one or the other of her sons began to speak, then looked at me and thought better of it. Rev. Clarke closed his eyes, and I wondered if he was praying. Lady Arbury seemed calm and resolute, as if she was gathering her strength for the coming interview. I removed myself from the bed and stood against the wall, hoping to be out of the way.

Travers opened the door and announced Holmes and Gregson. As he withdrew, Marion Arbury entered, and I saw Travers exchange a look of approval with her. She blushed and resumed her seat beside her mother-in-law. Rev. Clarke rose and permitted Holmes to take his seat. The curate, a troubled look on his face joined me at the wall. Gregson stood by the door. Holmes said nothing, but I could see a grim set to his mouth. Lady Arbury looked at him resolutely. From all appearances, they were enemies, preparing for battle, each gauging the strength of the adversary and marshalling their defences. But no matter how strong a woman she was or how prepared she thought herself to be, Lady Arbury could not possibly have expected Holmes's first words.

"Lady Arbury, how long has your husband been forsaking every vestige of gentlemanly behaviour and striking you?"

The outcry that went around the room was a mixture of surprise, anger, horror, and fear. So varied were the reactions, I could not hope to register them all, as I myself was taken aback by the directness and rudeness of Holmes question.

"How dare you!" exclaimed Bradford Arbury, once he regained the facility to speak, but Holmes raised his hand and commanded silence.

"I am right, am I not, Lady Arbury? You have applied your cosmetics artfully, but they cannot completely hide the tell-tale darkening of bruised skin beneath."

Her voice quavered as she spoke. "I fell down the steps, Mr. Holmes," she said, but there was no certainty in her voice.

"Come, come, Lady Arbury. This won't do. I have found the evil out. The mark on your face was caused by no fall. You would have bruises on your arms or legs, perhaps, places where you tried to break a fall, but you would not have a bruise so placed on your cheek without further visible injuries on your head. I am an authority on such matters, I assure you."

Bradford Arbury, anger in his voice, said, "I should thrash you within an inch of your life!"

Holmes looked at him coolly. "I shouldn't attempt it, Mr. Arbury. It would not go well with you."

Bradford Arbury sputtered in fury, but he was quieted by his mother. "Bradford, please." She turned to Holmes. She had regained her calm, but she was now devoid of bravado, as if she had laid aside every weapon. "Yes, Mr. Holmes, you are correct. For the last year, my husband has used me shamefully. I... I have kept this secret to protect my children."

"You are a brave woman, Lady Arbury," said Holmes. "You have my admiration."

Marion Arbury chided as if hurt, "Mama-in-law, you should have told us."

"And what would you have done?"

Her daughter-in-law responded, "I... I don't know, but we would have done something."

"Yes, that was why I said nothing. I was afraid of what you might have done. And so, I did what was necessary." She turned to Holmes. "I have no choice now but to be honest. In the past year, Kenton has turned to violence when faced by the smallest inconvenience or if thwarted in his will. It was preceded by a withdrawal of his interest: in me, our children, our estate, church, and even his books. I assumed... I assumed he had found interests elsewhere. I am not the first woman who has lost the love of her husband to another woman, though I never thought it would happen to me. We had been happy together, especially when first married. I felt shamed, and I determined to bear that cross quietly." She looked at Rev. Clarke. "Your sermons in that regard have been most helpful."

"My sermons," the curate responded, "were never intended to excuse such behaviour in a husband and father."

"No, of course not, but they helped me nonetheless. And then, the first blow came. At first, he was as shocked and surprised as I, but soon, he came to think it was my due and his right." She turned to Gregson, "And this was why I murdered my husband, Inspector. I could not bear it anymore, and I feared he might turn his anger on our sons or my daughter-in-law. I was certain I would not be believed by our local sheriff, who seemed quite enamoured by my husband. I took matters into my own hands."

Her children looked at her, horrified and speechless. Beside me, the curate was visibly shaken. Only Holmes seemed unaffected by Lady Arbury's words.

Gregson looked awkward and unhappy. "Lady Arbury, I know I speak for everyone here when I say I am shocked and profoundly moved by your admission. Only a brute would use a woman so. But murder is murder. I don't know that any jury will convict you, but my duty is clear."

"Of course it is, Inspector."

But Holmes intervened. "One moment, Gregson. Let us not be too hasty. I think there are one or two matters that need clearing up before you put Lady Arbury under arrest."

She looked at him. "One or two matters, Mr. Holmes?"

"Yes. Lady Arbury, from where did you get the knife?"

Without hesitation, she replied, "Why, from the kitchen, of course. I am often in and out of the kitchen during the day, assuring myself that all is well. The knife was laying there, having been used for slicing vegetables. I removed it and secreted it in my room. I doubt that any of the kitchen staff remembers."

"I doubt it, too," said Holmes grimly. "How did you commit the murder?"

"When we left my husband at table, and after assuring myself that my sons and daughter-in-law were otherwise occupied, I retrieved the knife from my room. I returned to the dining room, hiding the knife in the folds of my dress. I made certain no one saw me re-enter the dining room. Kenton has taken very little notice of me for some time, and he feigned he did not see me then, no doubt to reinforce his position concerning my lack of consequence. I approached him as he ate. It was surprisingly easy to insert the knife into his back. I would have thought it would have taken more effort. He made a little grunt of … surprise … perhaps, and died."

There was a small silence as we all pictured the scene in our mind's eye.

"Lady Arbury, you claim you stabbed your husband while he was eating."

"Claimed, Mr. Holmes? I state it."

"But the chairs around the dining room, indeed, the one on which your husband sat, all are high-backed chairs. How could you possibly have murdered your husband in such a manner when the back of the chair would have risen well above his head? Your husband's back would have been protected by the back of the chair. You could not possibly have inserted the knife into your husband's back, an act, I assure you, that is not the least bit easy and requires a certain amount of strength and determination."

A look of irritation flashed in her eyes, but she only hesitated a second. In an even tone, she said, "I neglected to mention that Kenton sneezed, Mr. Holmes. During the convulsion, his back was exposed."

Slowly, Holmes began to applaud, each clap of his hand preceded by a pause. "Very nicely done, Lady Arbury. Very nicely done." He looked at Bradford Arbury. "That, Mr. Arbury, is how one lies convincingly. If it were not for the fact that I believe your father was poisoned, I might well have been convinced your mother actually committed the crime."

Had Holmes thrown a bomb into the room, his words could not have been met with greater consternation and chaos. Patrick Arbury exclaimed, "Poisoned!" Others made similar ejaculations of dismay and disbelief. Lady Arbury closed her eyes as if pained and leaned back into her pillows. Gregson observed their reactions quietly, but intently.

When the initial outburst of reactions subsided, Bradford Arbury spoke in a voice mixed with anger and disdain. "If my father was poisoned as you say, Mr. Holmes, why all this talk of knives? Why this needless deception? Why are you wasting our time?"

Holmes sternly replied in admonishment, "Needless deception, Mr. Arbury? The only needless deception here has been perpetrated by you and the members of your family in an attempt to frustrate justice. Three of you are lying to protect the murderer, and one of you has permitted the others to lie on your behalf. As to the knife, it did not make it into your father's back on its own. One of you put it there. Which of you is responsible for that artifice?"

The silence of the grave followed Holmes's question. They looked at each other and at Lady Arbury, who still lay in her bed as if exhausted. And perhaps this time, she was. I, who was only an observer after all, felt the weight of the successive revelations heavily, and they were not my own secrets being exposed to the light of day.

After permitting the quiet to continue for no little time, Holmes spoke again. "I conclude from your silence that you remain intent on doing everything in your power to hinder this investigation. Very well. Have no doubt: the truth will not be hidden. I have already made great strides in exposing the mystery surrounding this murder. While you were alone with Watson, the medical examiner arrived from London and will remove the body thence. From forensic examination, we will learn the nature of the poison, information I have every hope that will further indicate the guilty party. And I have found other small clues that will be investigated. You can save us all a good deal of time and effort if you will only speak openly and honestly now."

The three young people looked at each other again, confusion and uncertainty written on their faces. Lady Arbury at last opened her eyes. "We cannot help you further, Mr. Holmes."

"Then likewise, I can offer you no more aid, only the assurance that I will arrive at the truth. You have my word." My friend rose. "Come, Gregson. Let us leave them to their own devices and the dreadful certainty that I will uncover that which they want so much to remain hidden."

He rose and headed for the door. We followed, then stopped as Lady Arbury spoke. "Rev. Clarke? Jeremiah? Would you be good enough to stay?"

"Of course, My Lady." He glanced meaningfully at Holmes and myself, and I could see his face was troubled. As we left, he regained the seat Holmes had vacated. He took Lady Arbury's hand in both of his, comfortingly.

Outside the room, we saw Travers, who was waiting discreetly several doors down from his mistress's bedroom, with Constable Fiddick. Travers approached us. "This way, gentlemen. Permit me to escort you back to the sitting room." We followed him down the hallway and stairs until we were once again where we had started.

"Well," asked Gregson, "what do you think?"

"I think there is more going on here than meets the eye. They are hiding something."

Gregson grunted. "Figured out that much on my own."

Constable Penhale joined us. "Beg pardon, sir. Dr. Dunning says he is ready to take the body back to London for autopsy, along with samples of the food and drink from both the sideboard and Lord Arbury's plate. He is also taking the pieces of glass found by Mr. Holmes so they can be analysed chemically." Then he added, "Oh, Mr. Holmes also suggested we search the body. There were no bottles of any kind found in his pockets." I remembered the missing morphine and laudanum, and was thankful that Holmes had attempted to retrieve them. Their disappearance still worried me.

When Constable Penhale didn't leave, Gregson asked, "Something else, Constable?"

"Yes, sir. There is another curate here, Rev. Phineas Hambly. He came to provide solace and comfort to the family, or so he says. I told him Rev. Clarke was already in attendance, and he said he would wait to give his condolences to the family, two curates being one too many at such a difficult time, he said. Then, to my surprise, he asked if Mr. Holmes was here. When I said he was, he asked to speak with him."

Gregson looked at Holmes. "You know him?"

"Other than the fact that, two days ago, he called at my flat to engage my services, he is a complete stranger to me."

"Shall I have him leave?"

"By no means. He has known the family for many years. He may have information that will clarify one or two points. You will certainly want to hear what he has to say."

Gregson had Penhale bring the reverend to the sitting room we had used previously. We joined him there, and Holmes introduced him to Gregson.

"Scotland Yard! Here!" The old man seemed quite beside himself, and not nearly as calm and in command as when he had visited us in London. He all but wrung his hands. "I cannot believe that Kenton is dead, and murdered at that! It is all over Wenlock Edge and the surrounding hamlets. Mr. Holmes, when I called on you, I could not possibly have foreseen such a horrible end! I would not have thought Lady Arbury could be so violent."

Gregson said, sharply, "Here now. What do you know of this?"

The question stopped Rev. Hambly as firmly as any wall could have done. He seemed bewildered by it, and then I could clearly see his keen intellect, which I had noticed upon our first meeting, engage his thinking. He calmed considerably. "Well, really, I know nothing. No, I know nothing. I apologize. I just assumed that... I mean to say... I thought it likely...."

Holmes rescued him. "Inspector, when Rev. Hambly called on us, he had reason to believe that His Lordship was having an affair with another woman. He had spoken with Lady Arbury, and she admitted to him that she feared this to be the case. I believe that when he heard of the murder, he assumed Lady Arbury, pushed beyond endurance by her husband's infidelity, murdered him."

He breathed a sigh of relief. "Yes. That is indeed the case. It was most careless of me. I have known Adelia for almost two decades. I know she could never commit such a foul deed no matter what the provocation."

I thought the retired vicar might change his mind if he only knew what we did.

Gregson spoke. "But you know there is another woman? Do you know her name?"

Rev. Hambly took a deep breath. "No. No, I do not. Lady Arbury assumed there was another woman, and I thought it likely. But when put like that, I have no knowledge of such a thing. Indeed, it was in an attempt to acquire that knowledge that I called on Mr. Holmes. I know only that Lord Arbury would visit London, sometimes overnight, and provide no explanation for his visits. Lady Arbury assumed another woman, and I did as well. Even now, I can think of no other reason for such visits. But, no, I have no real knowledge of another woman."

"Can you shed any light on the events of last night?"

"Only in that I know that there was a marked change in Kenton's – that is Lord Arbury's – attendance in church and these unexplained visits to London. I know nothing else. I am mystified, indeed, deeply upset, by all of this."

"Do you know of anything else that might be of help?"

He shook his head. "No, I do not. But, please, if I can be of any help to Scotland Yard, I stand ready to provide it." He turned to Holmes. "Or you, Mr. Holmes. I am sorely troubled by this unexpected murder. Any resources I might have expended in the search for another woman, I offer now to bring the murderer to justice."

"That is most thoughtful, Rev. Hambly, but I have already been engaged by Scotland Yard to assist in bringing the murderer of Lord Arbury to justice."

A wry smile appeared on the reverend's face. "I appear once again too late to employ your services." He looked at Gregson. "May I stay here until Jeremiah leaves?" He added, unnecessarily, "I know the family."

"I'll inform the constable," he replied, "and I'll have him notify the staff."

"And, please," Rev. Hambly repeated, "If there is anything I can do to make this ghastly situation any better, you have only to ask."

We left him in the sitting room.

Once alone, Holmes asked, "Gregson, may Watson and I accompany the doctor back to town on his way to the station?"

"Don't see anything against it."

"And I have one further request. May I accompany the body back to London?"

Gregson seemed as surprised as I was by the unexpected request. "If you wish. Are you giving up the case, Mr. Holmes?"

"In no way. I have enquiries that can only be made in London to test a little theory I have developed. I estimate that I will return tomorrow before the day is done."

I asked, "Holmes, am I to remain?"

"If you would do me that favour, Watson. I would like you to keep an eye on developments. Talk with the current curate and his wife. They know the family, perhaps not for as long as Rev. Hambly, but more recently, and their insights may shed light on the family's inexplicable taciturnity more than he could do. Gregson?"

"Yes."

"May I suggest a line of enquiry for you?"

"I hired you, Mr. Holmes. I'll hear your suggestion."

"I have two. Ask the staff about the knife. When was it last seen? Who saw it last? When was it missed? *Was* it missed? And then the broken pieces of wine glass. Who removed them? Where are they now? Questions on these topics, coming from those with the authority to command an answer, may elicit further revelations that will clear up this puzzle."

"Very good, Mr. Holmes. I had already decided to pursue those very lines of questioning."

"Good man, Gregson. Doctor?" Holmes indicated that I should follow him. We left Gregson to follow Holmes's suggestions as well as any other lines of investigation that might occur to him. We did not know then that future events would make information gleaned from those enquiries pointless.

Constable Fiddick followed us. "The coach is outside, Mr. Holmes, Dr. Watson."

"Thank you, Constable," said Holmes without slowing his pace.

"Mr. Holmes?"

At Fiddick's voice, Holmes stopped, and I with him. "Yes, Constable?"

Fiddick seemed uneasy. "How *did* you know, sir, that I was called away from my family so hurriedly?"

Holmes smiled. "Elementary. When I see a man who polishes the buttons of his uniform, as you do, but whose boots remain without shine, then I know I have met a man who was called away to work unexpectedly with insufficient time to shine his shoes. And when I further observe that your uniform, so assiduously cared for in every other way, has pockets that are ever so slightly deformed, I conclude that it is a result of overloading them with sweetmeats or other delights for his wife and children on his way home from work. Am I right, Constable?"

His amazement was evident. "Blimey! You're a ruddy magician!"

"Hardly, Constable. I am simply a man who not only looks, but observes, and not only observes, but deduces. Any one of you could do the same."

I, however, was not convinced that there would ever be anyone the equal of Sherlock Holmes.

Chapter 12

Holmes left for London on the afternoon train, leaving me with the vaguest of instructions. "Keep your eyes open, Watson, and your ears. If possible, I would like to know more about the lights that have been seen in Waltham Abbey. As I mentioned before, talk with Mr. and Mrs. Clarke. Discover what they know of Lord and Lady Arbury and their family."

"What am I looking for Holmes?"

"Do the lights only appear at the abbey? Do they only appear on Friday nights, as previously stated? Are there no other nights during which the lights are seen? What were the relations between Lord Arbury and his family and, now that he is dead, between the surviving family members? In short, learn all you can. Concentrate in particular on anything out of the ordinary, or a fact that fits no pattern."

"Holmes, I don't know that I can do this."

He seemed surprised, and then he placed a comforting hand on my shoulder. "Of course you can, old boy. I know of no one else who can do better."

His praise warmed me, no matter that I considered it unjustified and his trust misplaced. I resolved to do my best, knowing full well that I lacked his powers of observation, concentration, and deduction.

"I will return tomorrow. If all goes well, I will have the solution, and we can return to London the next day, on Saturday morning, in good time to surprise the future Mrs. Watson."

And so, that Thursday afternoon, I watched in front of The Good Lady as the carriage conveying Holmes, the medical examiner, Constable Fiddick, and the body wended its way down the main street and thence to the railway station. I was conflicted. I was fearful to be entrusted with so mysterious an investigation and anxious to see my friend return, but equally determined that I would wrest some nugget of information to aid him in bringing this puzzling investigation to a successful conclusion.

After a moment of hesitation in front of the inn, I decided I would do as Holmes suggested and visit Rev. and Mrs. Clarke, who had hired us after all, to learn from them if they knew anything of the Arbury family that would aid our investigation.

I was glad that I had brought a heavier coat, for the afternoon already promised a chilly evening. The walk to the vicarage warmed me, and I was further warmed by the greeting from Mrs. Clarke.

"Dr. Watson! Please come out of the cold. Let me relieve you of your coat. Jeremiah wanted to talk to you, and Phineas is here, too." I was heartened. Working together and pooling our knowledge, we might uncover a clue that would aid my friend.

She ushered me into his study, where I found the young vicar sitting at his desk and looking extremely distraught and haunted. Rev. Hambly was sitting opposite him, perhaps attempting to bring comfort to his young successor. Mrs. Clarke took one look at her husband, informed us she would bring tea, and left to fetch it.

"Dr. Watson, I am pleased to see you. Is Mr. Holmes not with you?"

"He has gone to London to make enquiries incidental to this case, and he has left me here in his stead. He expects to return tomorrow."

Rev. Hambly said, "I pray he has success."

The vicar rose from behind his desk and motioned the two of us to sit in one of the chairs to the side of the room. Although it was not yet dark, he lit the lamp on the table. Mrs. Clarke brought the tea, a welcome treat after such a long walk and joined us.

Finally, Rev. Clarke spoke, "Doctor Watson, the revelations made today have upset me tremendously. I would not have thought it possible for such brutality to exist. Even the holy scriptures, so honest about the fallibility and sinfulness of man and which describe and proscribe forceable intercourse in the frankest of terms, even they lack a like example. That any man could treat his wife so, and for it to happen within riding distance of my church without the least suspicion of its existence, saddens me to the point of despair."

"Jeremiah," said his wife with concern, "you must not blame yourself so. Of course he hid what he was doing. It's wicked."

Rev. Hambly nodded his head vigorously. "I, too, had no idea, and I knew them far longer. There was never a hint, never a suspicion of such abhorrent behavior."

"I agree," I said to Rev. Clarke. "There is no blame that falls to you for this."

He looked at me, grief still plainly written on his face. "Isn't there? Are you certain? I am not. A pastor should know his flock, but I did not know this. Why did she not say something? Did she misapprehend my reaction?"

"I think, rather, it was misplaced shame, and perhaps pride, that prevented her from apprising you of the situation, not any fear of your response."

He shook his head, "I have never spoken against such ill-use from the pulpit. Perhaps, had I done so and explained the evil of using a wife so, he would have been warned against such behaviour."

Mrs. Clarke said, "That would only be the case if he heard your words and heeded them."

Rev. Hambly added, "It would never occur to any pastor that such an admonition would be required among Christian men. Such abuse is abominable. I still find it difficult to believe."

After a moment of hesitation, I said, "I hope you will forgive me if I presume upon our short acquaintance. Rev. Clarke, you are a man of the cloth, and I, a man of science. It might seem that we have little in common, but would you permit me a question? As a doctor, I learn as much as I can to cure the physical ills that all men must face, at one time or another. Would you fault me if a man, woman, or child fell ill, and I could not cure them because I lacked knowledge that, if only I had studied harder or been more widely read, I would have known and could have used to heal them?"

He looked at me. "I catch your meaning, Dr. Watson. No. Of course I would not fault you. You are only human. You cannot know everything."

"Then I would say, neither can you. Had I not heard Lady Arbury herself, I would not have believed that any man could use a woman so, except perhaps among the meanest of our race who are barely worthy of the name 'man'. I cannot fault you for failing to speak against something that, in your innocence, you could not imagine."

I was embarrassed to see that Mrs. Clarke was looking at me with tears of thankfulness in her eyes, and Rev. Hambly as if he were seeing me in a new light.

Rev. Clarke said, "You are a good man, Doctor."

"I hope to be, Rev. Clarke."

The curate rallied, though a shadow of his earlier grief remained. "Perhaps I should thank the hand of Providence that I asked you and Mr. Holmes to come to Wenlock Edge. While I am embarrassed now at my reasons for that invitation, I am thankful you and Mr. Holmes are here."

"If anyone can bring a solution, it will be Mr. Holmes."

"Having heard and seen him in action today, I well believe it." He added, "Apropos to that, he must concentrate on this heinous murder and abandon the investigation for which you originally came. I will not be the least put out."

"Holmes believes the two are related."

All three of them showed surprise, and Jeremiah Clarke said, "Really? I do not see how that is possible."

"I believe he has his reasons," I said, uncomfortable with the necessary evasion. I was uncertain that Holmes would want me to reveal his discovery of the footprints and their possible relationship with Lord Arbury, even to the couple who had first brought us to Wenlock Edge.

The young curate shook his head. "This is all beyond me."

"And me as well. You must put your faith in Mr. Holmes."

He smiled wryly, and his soft answer took the sting out of what might have been a rebuke in another man's mouth. "You will forgive me if I put my faith in God, instead."

I suspect I blushed from embarrassment at such an obvious faux pas. "Of course. I did not mean to suggest otherwise."

"But I did not mean to discomfit you by correcting you. I beg your pardon."

Mrs. Clarke admonished her husband, "Jeremiah, you are impossible! Look what you've done! You've made Dr. Watson feel uncomfortable. You must apologize at once."

"I just did. Were you not listening?" He assumed so innocent yet so mischievousness an air it that I burst out laughing.

"See," he said, in mock justification, "Dr. Watson has forgiven me."

His wife retorted, "Only because he is a gentleman and not because you deserve it."

But I could see that for all she sounded stern, what passed between them was good-natured teasing. It was clear that they were very much in love, the proof of which followed as we all four laughed together. When we were finished, the Jeremiah Clarke grew solemn again.

"I fear that despite your kind words, recent events weigh heavily on my mind. Is there any way we can help you and Mr. Holmes? I am pleased that you have visited us, for both Margaret and I have determined to help you and Mr. Holmes in any way we can. I know Phineas is of the same mind, for we were discussing this before you arrived."

"I am gratified to hear it, and we would greatly appreciate any information you can provide. In fact, one reason I paid you this visit was to ask for such help. I consider it fortunate that Rev. Hambly is here, too. Mr. Holmes saw that you were in the confidence of Lady Arbury, and he thought you might know something about the Arbury family that might shed light on the unexpected murder of His Lordship, without betraying those confidences, of course."

He nodded. "Lady Arbury and her family regularly attend services in our church. They are very devoted."

"But Lord Arbury does not?"

He answered slowly. "No. I understand that, prior to my arrival, he attended with his family under Phineas' teaching. Isn't that right, Phineas?"

Rev. Hambly nodded and said to me, "I told you and Mr. Holmes as much, Dr. Watson.".

"I remember," I said in acknowledgement.

Rev. Clarke continued. "The Arbury's have a pew, of course. When I arrived, Lord Arbury attended only a few of the services that I conducted, and then ceased coming."

Mrs. Clarke said, "It was very strange, Dr. Watson. Once or twice he seemed to take umbrage at something my husband said during the message. His reaction was so violent that other members of the congregation remarked on it. Their pew being in the front, it was impossible for those behind them not to notice. And yet, no one listening could understand what my husband might have said to elicit such a reaction."

"Within a month," continued the curate, "he no longer attended services."

"I am as mystified as any as to why he would stop attending," supplied the older curate. "I am aware of nothing that would account for such a stark change."

Mrs. Clarke continued. "He did not even join us on Christmas or Easter. It was a great scandal in the village, for while we have some in Wenlock Edge who have never attended our church, Lord Arbury had always done so. As we said, his family members remain supporters of the church and parish and still attend services."

"And Lord Arbury gave no reason for this change in his behaviour?"

It was Mr. Clarke who answered. "None. After a time, I called on him at Arbury Hall to determine if I might have inadvertently offended him. At first, I thought he would not see me. Travers informed me that His Lordship was not at home, a patent euphemism for Lord Arbury being uninterested in giving me an audience. But then, as if he had reconsidered, Lord Arbury appeared. He abused me using the most profane language, declaring that I was a hypocrite or a covetous, pusillanimous fool to preach the drivel – he used that word – as if I believed it. He compared me unfavourably with Phineas who, he assured me, knew which way was up and understood the way things really were."

"That is an odd turn of phrase. What did he mean by that?"

"I have no idea."

"Nor I," added his predecessor. "I have heard many of Jeremiah's sermons, and they are as orthodox and edifying as any in the Church of England." He compressed his lips and shook his head. "There is no sense to this."

The younger curate continued. "He informed me that I was never to darken the doorway of his house again. 'I cannot stop my wife from attending your fairy meetings, but I can and will forbid you from forcing your superstitious and credulous religion on me in my home.' I omit some of the more offensive words he used. Travers, who stood stiffly and uncomfortably nearby, was quite pale. He and most of the town join us every Sunday, and I could see that his master's unwarranted treatment of me, overheard by passing staff, mortified him deeply."

"I can barely conceive that he could be so rude, save that he also turned me away at his door," said Rev. Hambly. "I begin to wonder if he might have been unbalanced."

I asked, "What of Lady Arbury?"

"I can only repeat that Lady Arbury continues to attend services, along with her family."

"What of her relations with her husband?"

"I know nothing of them, and I was shocked to hear of violence between them."

Mrs. Clarke intervened. "Perhaps I can help you understand something of those relations, Dr. Watson. Many of our parishioners work at Arbury Hall, for there are few other employers in our village. When I visit families who have members who work in the hall, they sometimes confide in me in ways they will not with Jeremiah. I will mention no names, but some who have been in service at the Hall for many years spoke of a change in Lord Arbury that preceded our arrival in Wenlock Edge. Once kind and solicitous of his wife and children, and even the staff, he became colder and prone to speak in terms that, frankly, some thought cruel and heartless. His treatment of Lady Arbury, in particular, was far outside the bounds any gentleman would permit himself, though none knew of violence between them. Or if they did, they never spoke of it to me."

"I was equally in the dark," said Rev. Hambly, "but I now recall that I was invited less frequently to the Hall towards the end. I was readying to retire from the curate, and I gave it little thought." He was grim. "Even so, I do not see how I could have failed to notice such a change in Kenton. I rather feel like Jeremiah, that I have somehow been remiss in my duties."

Mrs. Clarke regained the thread of her narrative. "After our arrival, they said he worsened. He would often absent himself from the Hall for long periods of time, even late at night. Some visits took him to London for days. For all of these, he gave no explanation or account. Lady Arbury was forced to manage not only the house, but the fields and lands, for Lord Arbury no longer took an interest in them. Many of the staff believe that Bradford and Patrick Arbury have stayed in the Hall to help their mother run the grounds, in order to forestall their deterioration from neglect and preserve their inheritance. Their father treated them scornfully and spitefully, and any child with even a modicum of pride and self-respect would have left long ago, had not their love for their mother prevented them. There have been strong words and fiery scenes overheard, and some of those have been repeated to me. It was not a happy home. And yet, knowing all these things, I would not have thought it would end in murder."

Mrs. Clarke's recitation did more to confuse my thinking than to provide any enlightenment to my mind. "Was there a reason given for this change in Lord Arbury?"

"None, only that it happened by degrees. If there was a reason, it remains unknown." After a pause, she said, "One servant at the house lays the blame on books Lord Arbury would read, books that she said were odd and fearful, but I cannot see how that would bring about such a deterioration of morality."

From the lengthening of shadows in the room, I could see the sun was beginning to set. I could not help but feel I had learned nothing of value. Perhaps that opinion was written on my face, for Rev. Clarke said, "I see that we have been no help to you, Dr. Watson."

"I do not know. Perhaps Holmes can find a clue among what you have related. I confess that I am no further along than I was, though I thank you for everything you have said. I will relay this information to Mr. Holmes. Perhaps he will discern a pattern in it."

I was readying to take my leave, intending to return to The Good Lady and see what I could learn about the mysterious lights at the abbey, when an urgent pounding sounded at the vicarage door. We all started. Rev. Clarke was the first to react and rose quickly. The three of us followed him to the front hall. He opened the door, revealing a village youth, breathing heavily as if from a long run.

"Reverend, ye must come quickly! Little Lily Nithercott be gone missing!"

Chapter 13

What followed was one of the most strenuous and fearful nights of my life. Jeremiah Clarke, Phineas Hambly, and I snatched our coats and followed the lad back to The Good Lady in Rev. Hambly's carriage. Mrs. Clarke insisted on accompanying us. It was dark well before we reached the inn, and I found the thought of Lily lost in the dark disturbing. I could not help but wonder how this had happened. When we arrived at The Good Lady, the inn was in chaos. While it was full of people, no meals or ale were being served. Mrs. Nithercott was wringing her hands in deep concern, moving back and forth helplessly and mechanically. Dennis Kempthorne and Sherriff Hender were assembling teams of men into groups and assigning search areas. Lanterns were being readied. Most of those in the common room were men, but there were some older women helping to prepare them for the coming search. Presumably, younger women were at home caring for their own children.

When we entered, Mrs. Nithercott rushed to us. "Rev. Clarke, Mrs. Clarke, thank ye for coming! And Rev. Hambly, it be good to see ye."

Jeremiah Clarke answered for all of us. "Of course. What can we do?"

"Lily be gone. She were in the back, but she be gone now."

Although I knew what the answer had to be, I still asked, "Are you sure she isn't with friends?"

Frantic, the good woman replied, "She not be with anyone!"

Mr. Nithercott, his face lined with worry, approached his wife to comfort her and said to me, "We do not know what happened. She were perfectly safe outside in the back."

Seeing my confusion at his remark, Mrs. Clarke said to me, "The back of the inn has a large yard with vegetables and herbs, as well as a grassy area that can be used for play. The entire area is surrounded by a wall meant to protect the vegetables from animals."

Mrs. Nithercott said, "Dolly be there, but Lily be gone!"

127

The fact that Lily was gone but her beloved Dolly was not, chilled me more than words could say. "But if there is a wall, how could she have gone out?"

"There be a door, but it were latched. It still be latched." The implication was frightful to the good woman, but even more so to me, knowing what I knew of Holmes's investigation.

Someone I could not see exclaimed, "The mad monk's got her!"

Nithercott bellowed, "There will be none of that!" and then looked with concern at his wife.

Kempthorne said, "Aye. None of that be needed." But I could see his own eyes betrayed no small amount of fear at the thought.

There was no time to ask further questions. Kempthorne was saying, "Ye all have yer areas. If ye find her, carry her here to Dr. Gingell."

I saw a thin, older man with a medical satchel and eye glasses, and presumed he was the town doctor. He said, his voice stronger than one would presume from his appearance, "I will stay the night."

Mr. Nithercott said to his wife, "Be strong, Aggie. I be back with her, I swear."

But I could see on her face that as much as she wanted to believe him, she was unable to completely banish her fear, knowing that any assurance he could give could have no guarantee.

"Move out!" yelled Kempthorne.

The crowd of men began leaving the inn, but some stopped when I raised my voice. "Has Gregson been informed?"

Kempthorne replied, "The inspector? Aye. He and his men be searching the grounds around the Hall, and the servants be helping, though it be a goodly distance for a little girl, I'd have thought."

"Then I'm coming, too."

"Ye do not know the land. Ye'll only lose yerself."

"I'll join a group. I will be another pair of eyes and ears, and I'm a doctor." I lifted my medical satchel that I still had in hand from our visit to Arbury Hall. "She may need immediate medical care that I can provide."

"Aye," he agreed, but reluctantly. "If yer group finds her, that be a good thing."

"I'm coming, too," said Rev. Clarke.

"And me," said Mrs. Clarke.

Kempthorne regarded her with irritation. "Ye will only slow us down in those skirts."

Determined, she replied, "There is a little girl, lost, maybe in the woods, certainly frightened, and possibly hurt. I'll find a way to keep up."

Mr. Nithercott interjected, seeing that Kempthorne had a retort on his lips. "There be no time to argue. I be taking 'em with me and Neville."

And that was what we did.

It would take pages to adequately describe the frantic, worrisome hours that followed, and I condense them here so I do not burden the reader. Rev. Hambly remained behind to help the town doctor and provide solace for Mrs. Nithercott. The three of us followed Mr. Nithercott and Neville, his companion, first through the town, then into the wooded area around it that had been assigned to us. We called out Lily's name until hoarse and walked until our limbs felt like weights. Only Mr. Nithercott and Neville had lanterns, as their number was limited and other groups and already appropriated them. We stumbled through the woods, on occasion tripping over tree roots and sometimes falling, for it was very dark and the forest ground uneven. The lanterns Mr. Nithercott and Neville carried were a mixed blessing. Without them, we had no chance of success, but they cast unexpected shadows that sometimes obscured depressions in the ground or other obstacles. As Kempthorne had warned, Mrs. Clarke's skirts were a significant encumbrance in the brush. I could only admire her fortitude, especially as I began to wonder if my own wounds, remnants from my service in the Afghanistan, would not hinder us more than her attire. I began to ache abominably as the night progressed and the air grew colder, and I could feel my limbs stiffening. But just as Mrs. Clarke made no complaint about the difficult progress, I, too, said nothing, but grimly continued. The thought of Lily in danger made my own pain unimportant. But as the night wore on and we received no encouragement, I began to fear the worst.

When dawn finally turned the sky red, it revealed us to be a scraggly lot. Our clothes had tears, and scratches lined our faces and hands. Our eyes were red from attempts to see beyond the light of the lanterns and from our vigil. Nithercott came to a halt and stopped us with a gesture. "It be time to go back." His voice was worn and steeped in the deepest pain.

"Perhaps she was found by another group," I suggested.

He shook his head, haunted discouragement on his face. "They were to ring the church bell if she be found. She be not found."

Mrs. Clarke said, "Then why are we returning?" The brave woman seemed ready to continue, and my admiration for her increased. I confess that I was nearing the end of my strength. The pain in my leg and shoulder, exacerbated by the extended activity in the cold, was nearly as bad as when I first received my wounds. Rev. Clarke, too, was drooping. I had watched him solicitously helping his wife over some of the more difficult terrain, and he was a man better suited for study than physical exertion.

Nithercott's unwilling whisper could barely be heard. "We must regroup. Eat. Rest. So we can better find her."

Mrs. Clarke said, "No! We should go on!"

But Rev. Clarke put his arm around her. "Margaret, we will. But Ivor is right. We must rest. We won't help her if we pass by her because we were too weary to notice her."

The man named Neville said nothing, but he shook his head grimly.

It was a dispirited quintet that returned to The Good Lady. There we met with other groups who were equally discouraged. Mrs. Nithercott was serving meals of sandwiches to groups of men, providing ale without cost. There were few words exchanged. Lily was still missing. The enormity, and the likelihood of what it meant, weighed heavily on all of us.

To me, this all made no sense. Missing animals. A murder. And now a disappearance of a little girl. I had never doubted Rev. Clarke when he told us about his impression of wrong in the village, but events had now made his intuition indisputable. How all this could happen in a few short days was beyond me. It was worse than any nightmare I could conceive.

And then Dennis Kempthorne entered through the front door. His face was grave. There were other men behind him, but they made no move to enter the inn. Instead, could be seen through the door, which Kempthorne held open as if in invitation. "Ivor," he said. Nithercott turned to him, and Mrs. Nithercott put a hand to her mouth, for we all heard the deadly import behind his words. Nithercott touched his wife, and then walked to Kempthorne. The two exited, shutting the door behind them.

A murmur circled the room. Mrs. Clarke said to her husband, her voice lowered, "Jeremiah?"

He said, "I fear the worst."

No sound came from the outside. After what seemed far too long a time, Nithercott returned, Kempthorne behind him. Nithercott's face was stricken by grief, and his wife made a noise. "Aggie." He took her by the shoulder and led her back into the room.

Kempthorne informed us unwillingly, his voice low, "The Sheriff found her clothes. Lucky he got lost, or we might still be searching. They be torn. Bloody. Mostly missing. Ivor recognized 'em. There be no doubt. Some animal took her."

"Oh, no!" said Mrs. Clarke in horror.

There was nothing any of us could say, and then the wailing came from the back of The Good Lady, a keening of grief that pierced our hearts. And one by one, we left the inn.

Chapter 14

But the truth was, I had nowhere to go. Realizing the awkwardness of my remaining in the inn while the Nithercott's wrestled with their grief, the Clarkes once again extended an invitation for me to stay with them, but I shook my head. "Holmes planned to return today, and he will expect me here. I thank you for your invitation, but I must stay."

"I, too, must return home," said Rev. Hambly. "God forgive me, but there is little I can do in the face of such grief."

After more assurances from the Clarkes that if I changed my mind, I was most welcome, they departed with Rev. Hambly, who transported them back to the vicarage in his carriage. I carried my medical bag to my room, silently made my toilet, and sat wearily in my chair, my head whirling with conflicting and depressing thoughts. Lily had been such a charming, sweet girl, and her parents good people. Her death at the hands of an animal was unjust, even in a world that held so much cruelty. I was not so foolish as to regard this as in any way unique, but I could not fathom how any animal could have snatched her from a backyard surrounded by a high wall specifically designed to prevent an animal from entry. It must have been an animal far larger than any we had considered so far.

When I woke to the sound of rushing footsteps, I was surprised, for I had thought the pain to which I was subjected by the night's search would have prevented sleep. Both my leg and shoulder still throbbed, though not as badly. Stiffly, I rose. The declining light from the window and the hollow feeling in my stomach informed me that, as improbable as it might be, I had slept through most of the day, perhaps as much from emotional shock as physical weariness. And then the door to my room opened.

It was Holmes. "Quickly, Watson. What has happened?" I must have looked at a loss, for he added, "The inn is empty. Our hosts absent. What has happened?"

I began to relay in as few words as possible the tragic news of Lily's disappearance and the macabre find from the search.

"Fool that I am!" I could not recall when I had seen him with greater fury on his face. "Fool to ignore what was in front of my eyes! Fool to leave on a Thursday after I had seen the pattern! And now the child is in danger!" His eyes burned with anger when they looked at me, and then I saw another emotion writ there: hope.

"Did you say the clothes were found by the sheriff?"

Bewildered at the question, I said, "I did."

"Only clothes?"

"Yes."

"Then all may not be lost, Watson."

"But Lily…"

"… May yet be alive."

I am sure I goggled at him. "But the clothes…"

"Deception, Watson."

"You cannot possibly be certain!"

"No, but I think it likely. For all that, we must act quickly. Bring your bag."

A desperate hope rising in my breast, I quickly picked up my medical satchel and followed him as he clambered down the stairs. He rushed into the back rooms by vaulting over the bar, and I followed by running around it. Given the circumstances, his unannounced appearance into their living quarters was wildly inappropriate, but as I caught up to Holmes, I could see the mixture of shock and hope in the faces of the Nithercotts as Holmes said, "We have no time to waste. Your daughter may yet be alive. I must see the yard." He snatched a lit lantern from the table, and we followed him out as he examined the wall and door with its aid and the dying light of the autumn sky.

Finally, he said, "It is as I thought. She was taken from here. She probably opened the door for them, was overpowered, and one stayed behind to latch the door and climb over the wall here." He said this last, pointing at faint marks on the wall. He looked to the Nithercotts. "If we have a chance to save your daughter's life, we must act with all dispatch. Do you have a gun?"

"Aye," said Nithercott, a mixture of worry, surprise, and hope fighting for dominance on his face.

"Fetch it and bring it."

Holmes reached into his inverness and pulled out my Adams Mark III revolver. "When my fears were confirmed in London, I fetched both yours and mine."

I took my revolver and put it in my pocket. "Holmes, what is going on? How bad is it that you speak like this?"

"Come," he said peremptorily, and led me back through the house, where we were joined by Nithercott, carrying a rifle, and trailed by his wife. We followed Holmes out the door of the inn, where to my surprise, I saw a cart and horses waiting, and young Symes sitting on the bench holding the reins.

"Thank heaven I had the foresight to ask our guide to remain when I saw the empty inn."

Nithercott said, "I can get more men."

Holmes shook his head. "We do not know who to trust," he said in a tone that brooked no argument.

It was a chilling statement. Bewildered, I listened as he said, more to himself than to us, "We need to send for Gregson, but we dare not spare the time to do so."

I said, "Surely we can trust the Clarkes."

With a look to me, he said, "Good man, Watson. To the vicarage, Mr. Symes." We left Mrs. Nithercott in front of the inn, on her face the same mixture of emotions that I suspect we all felt.

Joseph Symes did not spare his horses, and we were there quickly. No doubt, Rev. Clarke and his wife heard the sound of the horses, for they met us at the door before Holmes could knock on it. Symes and Nithercott remained in the cart, but I could see both Clarkes glance in their direction. Jeremiah Clarke exclaimed, "Mr. Holmes, what on earth...?"

"I must ask you to go to Arbury Hall. Find Inspector Gregson. Tell him to meet us at Waltham Abbey. Tell him it is a matter of life and death. Let nothing dissuade him. He is to bring his constables, armed if possible, as quickly as he can. We don't have a moment to lose."

I added, "Holmes believes that Lily Nithercott may be alive."

Hope sprang in both their faces. Mrs. Clarke pushed her husband toward us. "Jeremiah, go with them. I'll saddle Sadie and ride to the Hall." And I remembered that as a daughter of a peer, she probably rode as well as any of us, and almost certainly better than her husband.

Jeremiah Clarke offered his wife no argument. Instead, he followed her direction and pulled his coat off the coatrack beside the door as his wife dashed to the back of their home and, I presumed, to their stable.

"Do you have a gun?" Holmes asked him.

He raised his eyebrows in astonishment. "Of course not."

"Unfortunate," Holmes said, whirling and running to the cart. We sprinted after him. As we reached it, he said, "Rev. Clarke, this may be extremely dangerous."

"So I gathered. I don't understand, but I don't care. One man more may be the difference between success or failure."

"Very well." Holmes said to Symes, "As quickly as you can, we must reach the abbey. I will tell you when to stop, for we must approach it with our quarry unawares or run the risk of them disappearing, or worse, harming the child."

Symes did not whip the horses, but they understood him well enough to start at a gallop.

Holmes said, "I would not ask this of you or your horses, Mr. Symes, if time were not so critical."

"Aye," said the boy, keeping his concentration centred on his horses and keeping them safe as they galloped as fast as possible through the darkened path to the abbey.

"Holmes," I asked, "can you tell us now what is happening?"

After a pause as if he was weighing his response, he said, "We have the time. Yes. And it is best for all of us to know what we face." He turned to look at Rev. Clarke. "What would you say, Mr. Clarke, if I were to tell you that you have in Wenlock Edge a determined group of Satan worshippers?"

Even in the darkness, I could read the disbelief on the curate's face. "I would say you are mad."

"But I assure you, it is the only solution that makes sense of the disappearances." And then again, he railed at himself. "Fool that I am! I should never have left on a Thursday. I should have anticipated that the murder of Lord Arbury would accelerate their schedule."

His voice still rich in incredulity, Clarke said, "Are you saying Lord Arbury was involved in Satan worship?"

"Or I miss my guess," said Holmes, "and I rarely miss my guess."

I asked, "Holmes, how do you know all this?"

"I will explain my reasoning later. We do not have time for lengthy explanations. For now, this is what you all must understand. There may be twelve, possibly more people at the abbey. I would expect Lily to be alive, but drugged. She is in utmost peril. This group is mad to the point of evil as pure as any I have ever encountered in my career as a consulting detective. When my investigation led me to consider it as a possibility, I at first summarily rejected it as impossible. But I was wrong. This sect believes animal sacrifice will give them power and wealth, and they believe human sacrifice will be even more efficacious to that end. This is why you have missed animals, and why they abducted Lily Nithercott. You must be prepared to see friends among their number. Almost certainly, Sheriff Hender is a member, and possibly Mr. Kempthorne, though I am less certain of that. But remember, no matter who you see, they are not your friends, nor are they there by accident. You must be prepared to defend yourself – and kill if necessary – to keep Lily alive. Is that understood?"

"You frighten me, Mr. Holmes," said Rev. Clarke.

"Good. Then you will be careful."

"This is unbelievable," I said.

Holmes muttered, "I found it so, too, and ignored the possibility for too long." He added bitterly, "And I call myself a detective."

Ivor Nithercott asked, "Why did they choose my Lily?"

Holmes roused. "I suspect because you faithfully attend services at the church. Would I be correct?"

"Aye, that we do, but many do."

"Yes, and I suspect that is the link between all the families that have missed animals: they all faithfully attend services."

"Good heavens," breathed Rev. Clarke. "That is true. Ivor is a deacon in the church. So is Gresham. Bradshaw is an elder. The other families are equally involved in parish life and not mere congregants."

Thanks to Joseph Symes skilful driving and the strength of his horses, we had been making good progress. At a bend in the road, Waltham Abbey became visible. "Look!" said Nithercott. We could all see it. The abbey was surrounded by weird lights of various colours, and menacing shadows danced along its walls. My heart thudded in my breast at the sight.

"Ignore it," said Holmes dismissively. "It is only lanterns with stained glass instead of clear glass in the panes. They are carried either by hand or on poles, and there are cutouts held close to the glass to induce shadows and frighten the townspeople. It was more than the passage of time that removed all the stained glass from the windows. When I examined the walls of the church and the ground around it, I could see clear marks of the ladders used to provide access to them."

I could not help but think how effective a stratagem it was. Even acknowledging Holmes's explanation as probably correct, I was filled with no little apprehension, not to say fear. It was an unnatural sight.

After only a few more minutes, Holmes announced, "We must stop here and proceed on foot. We want to give them no warning, not only for our own safety and to ensure they do not escape, but to be certain they have no chance to harm the child. Make no sound, but be ready to act on my signal."

Joseph Symes stopped the cart. His horses were lathered, and he was forced to rapidly pass a rag over their flanks. As he tied them to a tree branch, Holmes withdrew a rifle from behind the bench and handed it to him wordlessly. As carefully and soundlessly as possible, we approached the abbey on foot.

The lights that had surrounded the abbey were all inside it now, but their odd assortment of colours and shadows still shone and moved inside it as if alive. The sound of chanting reached our ears through the open door of the church. The makeshift barrier was leaning against the church wall, and its doors were open. Holmes put a finger to his lips. While still outside, he motioned with his hands indicating that, upon entry, Rev. Clarke and I were to go to one side of the church, and Symes and Nithercott to the other. We entered silently, spreading out as Holmes had directed. He, himself, took the mid-point of the arc we created.

A weird and terrifying spectacle met our eyes. There were figures of various heights clad in long monks' robes with the hoods drawn over their heads. They stood in a semi-circle, hands outstretched beside their bodies, their backs to us, and their voices united in an unearthly chant, in which I recognized some Latin words from my schooling. As Holmes had thought, lanterns rigged with coloured panes and cutouts cast shadows of different shades in the room, creating a collision of eerily flickering silhouettes. Many of the lanterns were suspended by poles that were wedged in holes dug into the flooring. One figure stood apart from the others on the side of the alter. Even though he had his back to us, I could clearly see he was holding a knife. The small, unmoving form of a small child was on the altar. The intention of the figure holding the knife was clear, and my heart nearly stopped in horror. Was Lily merely drugged as Holmes had predicted, or was she already dead? Were we too late?

With a movement, Holmes caught our eyes. He nodded. There was no need for him to tell us what he now needed to do. I removed my revolver from my pocket and with a look to Rev. Clarke, handed him my medical satchel to better free me to shoot reliably.

At that point, the man at the altar turned as if to speak to his congregation and saw us, surprise appeared on his face. But it was no less than the surprise on mine. It was Rev. Hambly.

"We are discovered!" he shouted, pointing

There was a full-throated outcry. At first, I thought there would be no need to fire my gun, for the first impulse of the gathering was to disperse and flee like rats discovered by the sudden revelation of light. They began to run for various exits I could not discern, but then one of their number, who I abruptly recognized as Sheriff Hender shouted, "There are only five of them!" As one, they stopped their flight, turned, and led by some of their hardier number, they ran to attack us.

Holmes and I, having revolvers, were the best prepared to defend ourselves, as we could fire multiple rounds without reloading. Symes and Nithercott were less flexible, but we were fortunate that few of our opponents had firearms with them. But few was not all. I saw Hender clumsily lift his robe and reach to his waistband. Holmes shouted a warning, but when it was disregarded, he fired. Hender fell to the ground, writhing. At that point, another robed figure reached Holmes, and they began grappling for control of his revolver. Emboldened by the first attackers' success, the entire company rushed upon us.

A voice cried out, "Do it now!"

"The child, Watson!"

My attention drawn back to the altar by Holmes's shout, I could see Hambly at the centre of the group, the knife raised, rushing toward the prone, unmoving figure resting on it. I raised my service revolver and fired. A moment later, I was brought to the ground and onto my back by an attacker to turned out to be a woman and whose face was twisted with hatred and fury. She attempted to rake my face with her nails, and I raised my hands to protect myself. Suddenly, I saw, behind her, Rev. Clarke swing my medical bag, striking her on the head. She rolled off me, dazed, and the clergyman appeared horrified by his own violence.

I pushed myself to my feet as another cowled figure brought the vicar down and two more started in my direction. Hambly, still alive, was on his knees, perhaps searching for the knife that he had dropped when I shot him. I determined to give him no time to find it, and fired again. His body jerked and collapsed, unmoving. A cry of dismay broke out from our attackers, and they faltered.

Even with that, it might have gone badly for us, but at that moment Gregson arrived with Constables Penhale and Fiddick, closely followed by Bradford Arbury, Travers, and several other men I presumed came from the Hall. Their numbers turned the tide in our favour, and soon, all the robed worshippers were subdued and disarmed. None of their number were dead, though I would learn later that my aim had proven true and Hambly was stricken by two bullet and severely injured, perhaps for life. I was never so pleased to inflict harm on another human being. I took my medical satchel from Rev. Clarke, who still seemed dazed from his foray into violence, and ran to the altar. Lily was still unmoving. Her fingers and lips were a purplish-blue, and despite the loud commotion, she had remained unconscious. With apprehension, I recalled the article in the medical journal I had read that detailed symptoms of morphine or laudanum overdose.

Nithercott reached me. He was holding his right arm at an odd angle and was in obvious pain. Despite that, he had eyes only for his daughter. "Lily! Lily!" He tried to shake her gently with his left hand, but she made no movement. He looked at me. We were soon joined by Holmes, Gregson, and Clarke.

"How is she, Watson?"

"She is alive, but I fear she has been given a significant dose of morphine."

"But she'll wake up?" asked her father.

I pressed my lips together, for they were all looking at me imploringly. I was forced to speak the truth. "It depends upon how much she has been given. She is so small. They may not have accounted for that when administering the morphine."

"But after all this, she'll be alright, won't she? Certainly?"

When I didn't respond, Holmes said, "Watson?"

I shook my head. "I do not know."

"Can ye do nothing?" asked Nithercott, in more than physical agony.

I replied with reluctance and deep regret. "We are only just now understanding the dangers of morphine and laudanum overdose. We as yet have no cure, and I have nothing in my bag that can be of help." I took a trembling breath. "Her body will either eventually expel the morphine from her system, or she will succumb to it." I looked at her father. "I am very sorry. There is nothing I can do. All we can do is wait."

"Well," said Rev. Clarke, who was sporting an eye that was blackening and swelling shut as I watched, "there is something that I can do. When there is no help from man, there is always help from God." He placed a hand on her frail body. "Dear Father, please have mercy on this child and on us."

Behind us, I heard Bradford Arbury shout, incredulous, "Patrick!"

I turned to look behind me, and I saw Patrick Arbury among the robed figures who were now sitting under the supervision of the constables and other men. He was looking with a combination of false bravado and shame at his older brother, and Bradford was looking at his younger sibling with the shock of realization. Travers was equally white with disbelief.

Nithercott, also seeing him shook his head. Almost as an afterthought because his main attention was rivetted by Lily's unmoving body, he said, "Aye. There were some I canna believe would do such things. Silas Bennet. Widow Shaw. Sheriff Hender. Rev. Hambly. Others."

And then, to my astonishment, Lily Nithercott stirred. "Papa?" Her eyes were open, and she was looking at her father, confused.

"Lily!" He took his daughter up with his good arm.

"The bad people took me," she said. "Dolly be very scared."

"It be well now," said Nithercott, nearly weeping. "It be very well now. Dolly be safe. She be at home."

Holmes looked at me, an eyebrow raised.

I replied to his implied question, "I have never been so happy to be so wrong. As I said, we know little of morphine overdose." And then I turned to her father. "Mr. Nithercott, let me look at your arm. That, at least, is something I can care for competently."

Chapter 15

Later that day, Holmes, Gregson, and I conferred in the common room of The Good Lady. We had finished a meal of lamb sandwiches and ale, with pan-fried potatoes on the side. It was, perhaps, not quite up to the standards of our previous meals in the inn, for the Nithercotts were doting shamelessly on Lily and Ivor Nithercott only had one arm with which to work, but it was good, solid fare, and welcome, especially for me who had not eaten since the previous morning. I had spent many hours well in to the night, tending wounds, Nithercott's arm among them. I had done what I could for rescuers and cultists, including Phineas Hambly, and I was able to confirm that he would live to stand in the assizes. I regarded it as a fate too good for him. After the terror of the night, we were now calm and relaxed, and I could finally look for an explanation from my friend.

"Holmes, I must ask: how did you arrive at your conclusion that a group of Satan worshippers was at work? Even now, I find the thought incredible."

Holmes face darkened. "So did I, and for that reason, I took too long to credit it."

Gregson said, "I'd be glad to know how this all tied together with the missing animals."

Holmes waved a hand. "That was elementary," he said, and Gregson started a bit and appeared affronted. After a moment, the inspector decided to ignore the implied but unintentional insult. He listened with interest as Holmes explained. "I was already considering the possibility of human agency when Mr. and Mrs. Clarke spoke to us of the missing piglet. A predator might savage a piglet, but it would leave traces. A man, though, might handle a piglet and leave the rest. At that point, I expected I would discover some rural, childish feud at the root of the disappearances."

"I remember we had talked of the possibility."

"But to my mind, it became less likely when I discovered a pattern of animals disappearing on Thursday nights into Friday

143

mornings. It seemed more likely that there was some reason for the pattern other than mere animosity, though it could not be ruled out. For instance, was the perpetrator free only on Thursday nights, and that accounted for the pattern? But the discovery of multiple footprints made that explanation implausible. There were too many to account for a local feud, I thought. Certainly, there were too many to keep it secret, and no reason for so many to convene only on a Thursday." He looked at me. "You may recall, Watson, my investigation of Blackie, the Nibleys' cat. I saw a depression near her normal sleeping place."

"Yes, Holmes, I remember, but could not see that it was important."

"I theorized that a bowl of milk laced with laudanum was laid out for the cat that night to make the animal easily handled, and then both bowl and cat were removed. But there were many footprints around the chicken coop and at other places where animals disappeared. Why were so many people involved? Why not simply kill the animals if it was a feud? The evidence spoke of a cabal or confederacy of some kind which needed the animals on Thursday, or perhaps Friday, but did not want to keep them long."

Gregson said, "So that's when you suspected a coven!"

"By no means," answered Holmes, and I could see Gregson was again a little put out by his response. "It was the bones we found at the abbey. They indicated a macabre ritual of some kind. One that, I assume, was left undisturbed by the coven to increase its potency, confident that the twin deterrents of the weird lights and seemingly inaccessible church would protect them from accidental discovery. The fact that it was a ritual was confirmed to my mind by the arrangement of the bones."

"In a circle, you mean?" I asked.

Holmes shook his head. "It only appeared to be a circle." He extracted a piece of paper from his pocket and put five dots in a circular pattern, equidistant from each other. Gregson and I looked at it. "Is that what you remember of the placement, Watson?"

"It is. The bones were placed in a circle, each the same distance from the next."

"Now, watch." He drew lines between the dots that represented the placement of the bones. When he was finished, he sat back.

"A pentagram!" I said.

"Yes. They form a pentagram. When I recognized that lines drawn between the bones would form a pentagram, I considered the possibility of some kind of occult gathering that was engaging in animal sacrifice." He shook his head. "I dismissed it as incredible. I should not have done so. It explained all that we knew. Worse, at the same time, another thought occurred to me that I dismissed even more cavalierly."

Gregson asked, "What was it?"

"Human sacrifice. I had noticed that larger and larger animals were selected by the cabal."

"I remember," I agreed.

"I could not prevent the thought: do they intend to culminate in human sacrifice? Could they be practicing on larger and larger subjects to gain confidence for the final blasphemy? I rejected the thought as bizarre."

"It *is* bizarre," agreed Gregson.

"It was a grievous fault to discount the idea, for it was a reasonable extrapolation given the evidence."

"What make you change your mind?"

"My investigation in London. You no doubt recall the return address on the corner of the envelope I rescued from the fireplace."

"I can't say I do," admitted Gregson. "Didn't seem it could lead anywhere."

"The legible portion was '4367 A'."

"Very well, but how did that help? It could have meant anything."

"It was placed where a return address might be written. There are few cities in England that have streets of such length that they would have over four thousand blocks, and fewer still whose street name would begin with "A". I reasoned that

London was the most likely – and perhaps the only – city that could meet that requirement. I went to London to confirm my theory."

He continued. "What I found shocked me to my core, and, Gregson, you well know I have seen enough in my profession to be difficult to shock."

"What did you find?"

"A quick perusal of my maps showed me that only Addison Terrace was long enough to accommodate so many blocks. A visit to 4367 Addison Terrace found me in a less reputable portion of town, and in front of a church that at first look appeared abandoned. I entered it and discovered signs of recent use, as well as occult books and paeans to "His Satanic Majesty." By that time, the conclusion would have been obvious to a child. Conversation with those in residence around the church uncovered the alarming fact that many animals had gone missing in the vicinity without explanation, followed by the disappearance of two small girls."

"No!" said Gregson. "Not in London!"

"Yes, in London. You will need to inform the local constabulary upon your return to Scotland Yard. The similarity to the pattern we found here chilled my heart and forced me to accept the unacceptable. I began the return journey to Wenlock Edge, only to discover that I was too late. Lily Nithercott was already missing and presumed dead. I have said it before and I will say it again: I should never have left, not on a Thursday when I had already deduced a pattern. And I should not have so carelessly dismissed a theory that explained all we knew simply because I found it distasteful and unbelievable."

"But how did you know she was still alive?" I asked.

"As I admitted then, I did not know, Watson, but I presumed that she would be kept alive for the ritual, a ritual normally held on Friday nights at the abbey. They had done their best to prevent the curious from interfering."

"The story of the mad monk."

"Precisely. And when I learned that only Lily's clothes were found and not her body, and that they were found by a man I suspected to be involved in this occult league, I had reason to hope it was a subterfuge to prevent a wider search."

Gregson asked, "What made you think he was involved?"

"You will recall Sheriff Hender knew the substance of our conversation with Lord Arbury."

"He said it was overheard."

"He lied. As I said then, that portion could not have been overheard unless someone had been standing at the door, and I would have been aware of an eavesdropper. No, a more likely explanation was that Lord Arbury spoke with Hender either prior to our conversation, and the sheriff knew what the topic would be in advance, or shortly after our interview, and he was apprised of its substance after the fact. I suspected the latter, and that Arbury had handed him the items stolen from Watson's medical kit at the same time, which would explain why they were not found on his person. The coven had need of laudanum and morphine to keep their sacrifices tractable until the last, and they needed knives to remove flesh afterwards. My opinion that Hender was involved was confirmed when Lady Arbury referred to the respect the Sheriff had for her husband."

Gregson said, "And you suspected Arbury of being part of this coven...?"

".... Because of the match between his footwear and the footprints I had found at various animal abductions. I was confident of his participation even after my discovery that Bradford and Patrick Arbury wore footwear of a similar style."

I started. "They did?"

Holmes nodded. "I examined Bradford Arbury's footwear when he first spoke to us, and I positioned myself to see Patrick Arbury's footwear when I spoke with Lady Arbury. But despite their similarity in footwear, I was certain from his height and weight, that the footprints I had seen belonged to Lord Arbury. Bradford Arbury would have left footprints of a deeper impression due to his greater weight, and Patrick Arbury, being shorter, would have had a shorter stride."

I asked, "How did they kidnap Lily without anyone seeing them?"

But it was Gregson, not Holmes, who responded. "I can answer that one, Doctor. We had it from Lily. It was the sheriff. He spoke to her at the door in the wall and told her they had found Blackie, but he needed her help because Blackie was injured. When she opened the door, she was at his mercy. She explained that there were other men with him, and they put something over her face and she 'fell asleep.'"

"Probably chloroform," I said, wincing in sympathy. "How dreadful. She must have been terrified."

Holmes added, "In all likelihood, they then put her unconscious body in a bag and left, carrying her small form through the streets with no one the wiser. One of the more athletic of their number stayed behind to latch the door and then climb the wall. It was probably Patrick Arbury, for I saw signs of square-toed footwear in the ground by the wall. This would make everyone more likely to consider an animal, for if they left the door unlatched, human agency would certainly be suspected."

I could not help but ask, "So, did Patrick Arbury take over for his father at his decease?"

Holmes said, "I doubt it, for he was not in the centre leading the ceremony. That honour fell to the Phineas Hambly, to whom I refuse to bestow the title of reverend."

"I still cannot believe it!" I said.

"Neither could Rev. Clarke," said Gregson. "Quite a shock to him, I gather." And then Gregson added, I thought a little cynically, "No doubt Mr. Holmes suspected him all along."

"Hardly that, Gregson, but returning from London, having discovered unmistakable proof of a deranged coven of Satan worshipers, I did wonder at Hambly's attempt to keep me in London. His reasons were plausible at the time, yet I had always considered the coincidence of two men from Wenlock Edge arriving at my lodgings in the same day, barely twelve hours apart, to be unexplained. Given the revelation of a coven, I was forced to at least entertain the possibility that he knew of the Clarkes' visit and was attempting to divert me from Wenlock Edge."

"Did he?" I asked. "Know of the Clarke's visit, I mean?"

It was Gregson who answered. "That he did. We learned that much from Mrs. Clarke. They have village help. Effie Green, does for them. Seems she heard the curate and his wife talking about visiting you. She has a sister who does for Hambly, and she told her."

"And the sister told her employer?"

"No doubt. Hambly is saying nothing. Well, no matter. While many of these Satan worshipers are taking their cue from Hambly, some are talking. Some of the men and women – imagine, women doing this to a child! – some of them have told us that Lord Arbury was their leader. Hambly was second. Patrick Arbury joined them only lately."

"But why would they do this? What could they possibly gain from such heinous acts?"

"Power. Wealth. Or so they say. Can't believe it myself." He shook his head. "It's a terrible thing. Terrible."

"And possibly," Holmes added, "Patrick Arbury only joined in a pathetic attempt to please his father and gain his approval. Men can be very weak."

We were all silent, considering what we had learned. After a deep sigh, Gregson rose from the table. "Well, at least we have our murderer."

Holmes raised an eyebrow. "I beg your pardon, Inspector. You say you have the murderer?"

He smiled and grunted with pleasure. "Ah, I see Scotland Yard has got one up on you, Mr. Holmes. Yes. Patrick Arbury murdered his father so he could lead that cursed group. Guess he didn't expect Hambly to assume the reins. Thought being his father's son would be enough. Overestimated his chances, I think."

Now both eyebrows rose on Holmes's forehead. He was suddenly alert in his bearing, and his voice sharpened. "You don't say? Did he confess?"

"Course not." Gregson snorted. "Says he had nothing to do with it. Recanted his previous confession. Says he only did it to join in with the other family members and not look suspicious."

"Indeed. Who does he say murdered his father?"

"Claims he doesn't know, but says it was either his mother or his brother. Quite indignant, he is. Won't do him no good, of course."

"Because you don't believe him," stated Holmes.

"Would you?"

"I would prefer some proof to the contrary before dismissing his statement of innocence out of hand," Holmes said, his voice still pointed.

Gregson grinned at him good-naturedly. "Come, come, Mr. Holmes. You've had your little success here. You can't win them all. Let us in the Yard have a moment of glory or two."

After a short pause, Holmes leaned back in his chair, and I watched the tension leave his body as if by force of will. He smiled. "I see you've got me there, Inspector."

"Course I do! You can have the next one. I must meet the train. Got a bevy of constables coming to get this coven group to London, seeing how the law here was in cahoots with them." And he started to leave, stopping only to turn and say, "Oh, and the autopsy came back. Strychnine, as you thought."

"Were there traces on the shards?"

Gregson nodded. "As you suspected. And in the food, too."

Holmes was surprised. "In the food, too?"

"It's what the wire said. Taking no chances, he was." His face grew grim. "A British Lord and a curate of the Church of England worshipping the devil! Don't barely believe it, but there it is. What is the world coming to?" And with that rhetorical question, he left us alone in the common room.

We were both silent. I was watching Holmes. Immediately upon Gregson's departure, he resumed a keenness in his expression. He drummed his fingertips on the table.

"Holmes?"

"Watson?"

"*Did* Patrick Arbury kill his father?"

He looked at me and smiled. "I should be very much surprised."

"But then, who did?"

"That is not the question. That is obvious. But what is not obvious is the motive of the murderer, and how to account for the flurry of confessions. Rather an embarrassment of riches, I would say."

I closed my eyes and sighed. "And here I thought we were done."

"Soon, Watson. Soon. I must think on this. I cannot see how the murder relates to all we have learned."

"Neither can I, Holmes. It is as if they are two different cases."

Holmes abruptly stopped drumming on the table, remained unmoving for several seconds, then turned to look at me keenly. His gaze was sufficiently piercing that I found myself somewhat incommoded and discomfited by it. After a moment, he rose and put a hand on my shoulder. "Watson, if I am ever so inconsiderate as to forget your service and intimate that I alone can see to the heart of a matter, I beg you to remind me of this moment."

"Holmes, I have no idea what you are talking about."

He smiled again. "You will, Watson. You will."

Chapter 16

Holmes sent word to Joseph Symes, and the red-headed youth conveyed us to Arbury Hall the next morning. He had been knocked about quite badly by three of our attackers before we were rescued by Gregson and his men, but he was a stout lad and grinned at us cheerfully, no doubt proudly wearing his bruises as marks of honour from a battle. I was confident his friends would hear stories from his own lips about that night for many years, and no doubt his children and grandchildren after them. Our bags were packed and in the cart, for we were to leave for London on the afternoon train.

We had said our goodbyes to the Nithercotts earlier.

"We be not taking a farthing," said Mrs. Nithercott. "Ye saved our little girl."

"I disagree," said Holmes. "I endangered your child by my own stupidity when I disregarded obvious clues and left for London. You will take this money as recompense to assuage my conscience."

"It be too much," said her husband.

"It is just enough. Any less and I would not be able to look at myself in my shaving glass."

They disagreed for some time before Holmes finally imposed his will upon them. As they argued, Lily quietly approached me. "I be sorry to see ye go, Dr. Watson."

"And I'm sorry to go, too. I will miss you."

"Ye were very good to Dolly."

"It was my pleasure."

She sniffed a little bit, and I could see she was attempting not to cry. I feigned not to notice. "What if Dolly gets a cold? What be I doing?"

"I am confident that Doctor Gingell will see to her health." She looked dubious. "And you still have some of the powder I gave you, correct?"

"Aye."

"Then you will give her that."

When we left the inn, the looks the Nithercotts gave us plainly said they never expected to see us again, though I had my own ideas on that subject that I had not yet conveyed to Holmes. Young Symes conducted us to the Hall, his horses being none the worse for their exertion two nights previously.

As we alighted, Holmes said to our guide, "We may be some time. Will you be willing to wait?"

"Mr. Holmes, ye've paid me enough already for me to wait three days. I be here when ye be ready."

We rang the bell to Arbury Hall, and the door was opened by Travers, who barely controlled his surprise at the sight of us. "Mr. Holmes. Dr. Watson. How unexpected. We thought you had left with Scotland Yard." He managed to convey disapproval by the tone of his voice without actually descending to rudeness.

"Given all your household has endured the past several days, I regret the need to disturb you further, but we have unfinished business, I'm afraid. May we speak with Her Ladyship and the new Lord and Lady of Arbury Hall?"

He displayed only the hesitation of a moment. "Of course. Let me show you to the sitting room. I will see if the family is at home and able to entertain visitors."

He was as good as his world. We waited in the sitting room until Travers returned with the Arbury family, their faces displaying a mixture of wariness and concern.

Lady Arbury entered the room first. I still I thought of her as Lady Arbury despite the fact that the title would now belong to her daughter-in-law. Bradford Arbury, now Lord Arbury, and his wife followed her. Lady Arbury wasted no time. Like Travers, there was a note of censure in her voice. "Mr. Holmes. I must express some surprise in seeing you again. Surely, you have done enough." Suspecting what was to come, I could not blame her for being unhappy.

"I do beg your pardon, Lady Arbury. I appreciate your willingness to give us an interview. I give you my word, it is unavoidable. One moment, Travers," Holmes added as Travers began to close the door. He looked at Lady Arbury. "Please excuse my boldness, your ladyship. May Mr. Travers stay? Doctor Watson will not admit it, but I know by the way he carries himself that he the wounds he earned in the Afghanistan during his service in Her Majesty's army have been inflamed by his twin expeditions two nights running. He may have need of a restorative." She hesitated. "And Travers's attendance with us here may be helpful."

After a pause, she nodded. "Please, Travers."

"Very good, my lady."

I looked at Holmes. While it was true that my wounds had become inflamed, first by the futile search for Lily and then the next night by her rescue, and while it was true they were still painful, I could not imagine how any "restorative" would improve them. But I said nothing.

"Please, be seated," said Lady Arbury. Holmes and I sat on separate chairs. The two women sat on a settee, with Bradford, the new Lord of Arbury Hall, standing behind them. Travers stood by the liquor cabinet, presumably in the event I requested the restorative Holmes had mentioned. If their faces had betrayed any anxiety previously, it was now magnified tremendously. "I hope you won't be long, Mr. Holmes. Our family is grieving its losses: first, the death of my husband, and now the arrest of my youngest son for his murder."

"Then I can relieve your mind on that last score, Lady Arbury. Your son will not be convicted of the murder of your husband."

Holmes's words took her by surprise.

"He won't? How can you be so sure?"

"For the simple fact that I know he did not commit it."

Rather than relief, the looks of alarm they exchanged palpably increased the tension in the room. Marion Arbury put a hand on her mother-in-law's arm, as much to obtain solace as to dispense it. Bradford Arbury stiffened. Travers closed his eyes as if in pain. For his part, Holmes looked as alert as a cat with a mouse.

Finally, Lady Arbury said, "You seem very certain, Mr. Holmes."

"I am, your ladyship."

"But that inspector seemed quite sure that my son," and here her voice trembled, "murdered my husband to obtain a position of prominence in this league in which they participated."

"I am not so easily satisfied as Scotland Yard."

"I see that you are not."

Bradford Arbury, who had barely contained himself through this exchange, finally vented his frustration. "Enough of this, Mother. Let's toss him and his friend out on their ears and be done with them."

Lady Arbury partially turned to her son and touched him to still him before returning her gaze to us. "Bradford, you have much to learn before you can be as good a husband as my daughter-in-law deserves. I believe Mr. Holmes is correct." She sighed and put her hands on her lap. "How did you know?"

"It was rudimentary, Lady Arbury, particularly after Watson here helped me separate the disappearances and kidnapping from the murder. I suspect the murder would have occurred that night no matter what else might have happened before or after it, though I believe the murder of your husband accelerated plans for the sect that had been in motion for some time."

Marion Arbury looked to her mother-in-law. "Mama-in-law, what is he talking about?"

The older woman patted the youngest one's hands consolingly. "You are such a dear child."

The young woman looked at her husband, fear on her face. "Did... Bradford, did you kill your father?"

It was Holmes who answered. "No, nor did your mother-in-law, though that was what you were expected to think."

Again, Lady Arbury sighed. "I see you do know everything, Mr. Holmes."

The younger woman was visibly disconcerted. "But then, was this all for nothing?"

"This may go quicker and with less pain if I explain what happened."

"Please, Mr. Holmes," she said, agreeing.

"Mrs. Arbury, you believed that your mother-in-law murdered your father-in-law, and that your husband and brother-in-law confessed to the murder only to shield her, hoping Scotland Yard could bring no case to trial with so many conflicting confessions. And then, you joined them, hoping to add another level of confusion and protection."

The young woman said, "Ye-es."

"It might even have worked. And I can understand why you thought she had murdered your father-in-law. As she told Inspector Gregson, after your mother-in-law assured herself that you and her sons were otherwise occupied, she did return by herself to the dining room. She even carried the knife with her, having removed it as she said, but she only did so for protection. It was the reason her story rang so true, that and her motive. She had no thought to commit murder, the prohibitions against murder being too well established by her religious upbringing to disregard them. I suspect she intended only to declare herself ready to bear the scandal of suing for divorce and making her reasons public, unless he left the Hall and never returned. But upon entering the dining room, she surprised the murderer on his knees before the fireplace, cleaning up broken glass, and saw her husband dead at table."

The room was quiet to the point that I could hear their breathing.

"Of course, it was Travers who poisoned His Lordship."

Bradford Arbury spoke, "This is preposterous! How dare you enter our house and make these accusations against a trusted servant!"

But Travers spoke. "Master Bradford, please. It is quite alright. I am content and relieved the deception is at an end." He faced Holmes. "Yes. I killed the master."

"It was, of course, why you sent the staff away and served him alone. You didn't want anyone to see you administering the poison."

"You are quite correct. Having decided that the master was not fit to live, I determined I would not hang for him. As I served him, I added strychnine to both his food and his wine. It was the

156

wine that gave me away. He had eaten several bites of his food, angrily yet with evident relish, but he must have discerned something in the wine, taste perhaps, though I had informed myself enough to know that strychnine is reputed to be tasteless. How one knows the fact for certain, I do not hope to know. Or perhaps, he had begun to feel the effects of the poison. However it was, I could see the realization of my deed on his face, and he threw his wine glass at me. It shattered against the fireplace. He made a motion to leave the table, but he began to foam at the mouth and convulse." He swallowed. "It was quite disturbing to witness. No amount of information prepares one for killing another human being in so brutal a manner, no matter how deserving he was of it."

"And the letter I found inefficiently burned in the fireplace?"

"It was the letter that prompted my actions. It had arrived by morning post. I opened it as I did for all His Lordships mail. Upon doing so, several words caught my eye on the reverse side, quite by accident. But once I saw them, I could not prevent myself from reading the letter in its entirety. I had already been considering relieving the family of His Lordship's cruelty by the expedient of poison. I knew that the master was shamefully handling his wife." At this point, he turned to Lady Arbury and said, "You said nothing, of course, but such things cannot be hidden from a personal maid. Naturally, she informed me. Moreover, I had recently surprised His Lordship attempting to force himself on his daughter-in-law."

"What!" exclaimed Bradford Arbury, whose face went white with anger. "And you said nothing to me?" He turned to his wife, his voice equally filled with accusation as well as horror. "Is this true?"

"Please, Master Bradford, do not blame Lady Marion. There was no fault in her. His Lordship was no longer himself. I assured Lady Marion that I would handle things discreetly. Without giving my reasons, I instructed the staff to never leave Lady Marion unattended. I left the details of completing my instructions to Mrs. Durrant. I did not inform you of the deed for the same reason that Lady Marion did not. We were afraid of what you might do."

"I would have killed him!"

"Quite so. You would have done so without thought, brutally, leaving no question as to your guilt. You would have hanged, and Lady Marion would have had to raise your child alone."

I would have thought no man could go paler than Bradford Arbury was already, but I was wrong. The shock, happy though it was, turned his face bloodless. I rose quickly to help him to a vacant chair, where some of his normal colouring returned once he was seated. He seemed entirely speechless.

Travers coughed into his fist. "Sir, I do beg your pardon. I thought you knew." From the look on her face, Lady Arbury had suspected her daughter-in-law was with child and now had her suspicions confirmed. "It did make it easier for the staff to assume the reason for not leaving Lady Marion unattended were more benign than they actually were."

Marion Arbury said, weakly, "With everything happening...."

Holmes spoke. "No doubt one more thing that cannot be concealed from a woman's personal maid."

"Precisely, sir," said Travers.

"So, knowing these things, you were already planning murder."

"Indeed, sir. Someone had to act."

"And the letter. I assume it contained encouragement and justification for both animal and human sacrifices."

"As well as instructions on how to do it 'humanely,' as if such a thing were possible. I would prefer not to relate the details. They were most appalling and alarming. I decided I had tarried long enough. His Lordship's anger after his interview with you provided me a reason to dismiss the staff. Once I was certain His Lordship was dead, I took the letter, which I had in my possession for this reason, and consigned it to the fire, envelope and all. I dared not do it earlier in the event his Lordship missed it. Wording in the letter indicated he was expecting it. I then moved a glass from one of the other settings and placed it in front of His

Lordship's plate, then returned to the fireplace to retrieve the broken pieces of glass. It was at this moment that Her Ladyship entered."

Lady Arbury said, "At first, I thought Kenton had had some kind of seizure, and I admit that I thanked God for it, but then I saw Travers's face, and I knew what he had done. He admitted it to me when I confronted him."

"I presume it was your idea to implant the knife in your husband's back?"

"I thought it would prevent anyone from suspecting the truth, for I had no intention of allowing a servant as loyal as Travers to suffer for relieving us of our misery. I permitted Bradford to believe that I had killed Kenton, and confessed that I was being beaten by his father. It was difficult for him to believe, but I was able to show him many bruises that left him no choice but to accept what I said. It was Bradford who suggested that we both confess to the crime, which he believed would make prosecution difficult, if not impossible. Patrick joined us for reasons of his own, and then Marion. I gave Travers strict instructions to say nothing. It is harder to bring a lady to trial than a servant."

"*Noblesse oblige*, Lady Arbury?"

"As you say, Mr. Holmes."

"I am pleased to know that loyalty among gentry and servants goes both ways."

After a moment of silence, Lady Arbury said, "So what now, Mr. Holmes? Do you drag Mr. Travers off to London? I warn you, I will not renounce my confession."

"Nor will I," croaked Bradford Arbury, still recovering from the successive shocks of the interview.

"Nor I," said his wife.

Holmes smiled. "Well, that leaves us with a pretty problem, though perhaps not one that is insoluble." He looked at the butler. "Mr. Travers, I presume that your days as a poisoner are at an end?"

Travers was surprised by the question's implications, and he took some moments to consider his response. His face was grave. "You are correct, sir. It was a fearful thing I did, and I am not certain now that what I did was right. But with Sheriff Hender not to be trusted, I saw no other recourse. I will not take an action like that a second time."

Holmes nodded. "And, of course, you will have no need."

"There is that, sir."

Holmes then addressed Her Ladyship. "I do not see how the crown will obtain a conviction of Mr. Travers under those circumstances, and I am not certain that justice will be served if it tries. Scotland Yard seems quite happy with its suspect, and while I am certain your youngest will escape the hangman, I am afraid there is no doubt that he will serve many years in gaol for his part in the crimes of this coven. I am sorry, but there is no recourse for that."

With dignity, she said, "As much as I wish it were not true, I too see no other outcome. I will content myself with those who remain, and visit Patrick as I can." Her face twisted, and then she composed herself. "The corruption of my child is another crime to lay at the doorstep of my husband. Perhaps my son can be redeemed. Rev. Clarke would assure me it is possible."

After a pause, Holmes said, "I have one more thing to ask, and for this I do not have the answer."

"Ask it, Mr. Holmes."

"I have it from Watson that your husband was once loving and solicitous of you and others. What changed him?"

"I cannot answer that question, Mr. Holmes, for I do not know. It will forever remain a mystery, I'm afraid."

Travers cleared his throat. "If I may, I believe I can shed some light on the late master's motives. At one time, he was a great reader, and a book came into his possession titled *The Magus*. He seemed deeply affected by it. But I believe it was another, more recent book that seemed to turn him, or perhaps I should say, to turn him from the Church of England and make him more susceptible to other influences. The master insisted I read it. *The Origin of the Species*."

I started slightly, for I had heard of it, though I doubted Holmes had. I understood there was no little controversy surrounding it, though I had never heard of its reading leading to such dreadful actions.

But Travers was continuing. "I found the book quite preposterous, for it stated that we are not created beings, but mere accidents of nature. The master seemed quite upset by it, though perhaps incensed would be a better description of his reaction. He, in turn, shared it with the vicar, Rev. Hambly, and Sheriff Hender, though I do not believe the latter understood it. They shared it with others. I overheard His Lordship speaking with Rev. Hambly about its contents. Lord Arbury seemed angry that so many laws of morality were forced upon us for no good reason, but were lies perpetuated by the clergy, and he determined to find a new morality more in keeping with science. Rev. Hambly appeared to agree with him. He certainly offered no contradiction in my hearing."

"But he continued to attend services?"

"Until Rev. Clarke came. I recall the service in which the young vicar mentioned the very book from the pulpit, for his opinion of it agreed with mine. It was one of his first sermons, and one of the last His Lordship consented to hear. After that, there were other books, each more despicable than the last, with titles I have forgotten, save *Le Grand Grimoire* and *The Voynich Manuscript*. The maids were quite frightened of them, for the master would leave them about, open, and pages with disturbing illustrations were displayed for any and all to see. Perhaps he did so purposefully. I could not say. I believe it was these latter books that sealed the master's decline."

"Hardly books, I would think, that would incline one to a new morality founded on science."

"Quite so, sir. Quite so. I have already taken the liberty of burning them. I am pleased to no longer have them in the house. They were quite… inappropriate."

After a short silence, Holmes rose from his seat. I followed suit. He addressed Her Ladyship. "I thank you for your time, and I apologize for any distress I have caused you and your family."

"On the contrary, Mr. Holmes, you have set my mind more at ease than I would have thought possible. I am content that someone other than Travers and I knows the truth, and I believe I can trust your discretion, and that of Dr. Watson."

"Of that, I can assure you for both of us," responded my friend.

Leaving the three Arburys alone, we followed Travers to the front door, but before we left the doorstep, Travers said, "Please, accept my gratitude for your kindness, though I do not know that I deserve it."

Holmes responded, "There has been enough death and sorrow here, I judge. Matters such as yours, I leave for other hands than mine."

We ascended the cart, and Symes started for the station, chatting amiably about his not inconsiderable family and the antics of his younger brothers. For my part, I listened in silence, for I had proposed to speak with my betrothed, explain more fully why my absence had been necessary, and see, perhaps, if she would prefer our December wedding be held in a rural, village church instead of a service at the Register's Office.

Epilogue

As I have never previously written a prologue to any of my stories or books, neither have I before written an epilogue. But as it has never before been so long between the original occurrence of the events and my putting pen to paper, I fancied that, perhaps, the reader, if there is one, would want to know more of what happened to the personages found herein.

My betrothed, Mary, consented to be my wife at the church at Wenlock Edge, officiated by Rev. Jeremiah Clarke. The interior of the church, while it lacked the ornate woodwork found in London churches, was beautiful. Holmes and Mrs. Hudson attended, the former shaking his head when he thought none of us was looking, and the latter dabbing her eyes with her kerchief. Young Symes and the Nithercotts served as additional witnesses.

Those who participated in the coven received varying degrees of sentencing by the courts, with the most severe meted out to Phineas Hambly, who was subsequently defrocked by the Church of England. He died in prison after serving only part of his sentence. The London authorities investigated the coven found in the abandoned church on Addison Terrace, and its participants were arrested and received similar sentences. My friend, Sherlock Holmes, assisted them in procuring evidence and was called upon to give testimony in court.

While I have never returned to Wenlock Edge since my marriage, I have had some small but steady correspondence with Rev. Clarke, and then with Lily Nithercott. The former continues to serve at Wenlock Edge, now a more prosperous village than it had been when we visited. He has declined several attempts to promote him into the hierarchy of the Church of England, claiming that his calling is among those of the village. He and Margaret Clarke now have five children, three boys and two girls, whom I understand are much beloved. Despite having so many children and so many duties for his church, he has found time to read every account of my adventures with Sherlock Holmes, and he has kindly expressed his delight in my continued career as a biographer.

Ivor and Agnes Nithercott continue to serve meals at The Good Lady, and the inn has grown in clientele and popularity. As I write this, Lily Nithercott is nineteen years of age, and she writes me that one of Joseph Symes's younger brothers has shown no little interest in her.

Lady Arbury died not quite nine years after the events in this manuscript, but she lived to see her youngest son, Patrick, express remorse for his actions. The Rev. Clarke had no small hand in this welcome event, for he regularly visited Patrick Arbury in prison in an attempt, he wrote me, "to bring one of his lost sheep back to the fold." Upon his release from gaol, Patrick Arbury lived for a time with brother, sister-in-law, nephew and two nieces in Arbury Hall. Later, he repaired to London where he opened a concern dealing in artwork, small statuary, and other curios. I understand it is moderately successful.

As I related in the prologue, Holmes read the manuscript, convinced after his reading that his timely rescue of Lilly Nithercott did not sufficiently obviate him from culpability for endangering her unnecessarily. I remain of another opinion, convinced no man could have done more. Without him, she would have met a gruesome and untimely end. I find I cannot fault him, as he does himself, for dismissing the unbelievable despite so many clues, or for leaving on a Thursday when he had deduced a pattern of Thursday disappearances.

It is for you, the reader, who now is in full possession of the facts concerning a village darkened for a time by evil, to decide which of us is correct.

During his life, Barry Clay has dug ditches, cleaned bathrooms, and asked if you'd like fries with that. He is currently a first level supervisor and project manager for a Computer Design Agency with the federal government, the volunteer conductor of a local student Orchestra, the father of four children, "Opa" of one grandchild, and husband of one wife. He has been commissioned to write music, and his first two musicals were locally produced. His books, short stories, novelettes, and novellas are available in both Kindle e-books and printed form through Amazon and other booksellers.

Made in the USA
San Bernardino, CA
26 February 2020

65010495R00112